T0354972

A PERFECT
MURDER
TAKES TIME

Other Books by Marc D. Hasbrouck

The Murder Of Devon Stone
Another Word For Murder
Remember You Must Die
Murder On The Street Of Years
Down With The Sun
Stable Affairs
Horse Scents

A PERFECT MURDER TAKES TIME

A NOVELLA

MARC D. HASBROUCK

A PERFECT MURDER TAKES TIME
A NOVELLA

iUniverse books may be ordered through booksellers or by contacting:

iUniverse
1663 Liberty Drive
Bloomington, IN 47403
www.iuniverse.com
844-349-9409

Because of the dynamic nature of the Internet, any web addresses or links contained in this book may have changed since publication and may no longer be valid. The views expressed in this work are solely those of the author and do not necessarily reflect the views of the publisher, and the publisher hereby disclaims any responsibility for them.

Any people depicted in stock imagery provided by Getty Images are models, and such images are being used for illustrative purposes only.
Certain stock imagery © Getty Images.

ISBN: 978-1-6632-7074-0 (sc)
ISBN: 978-1-6632-7075-7 (e)

Library of Congress Control Number: 2025902276

Print information available on the last page.

iUniverse rev. date: 02/06/2025

<u>This book is dedicated to the various teachers</u>
<u>I've had throughout my life.</u>

Those who nurtured my creativity, those who encouraged me to explore, those who taught me to open my mind and to discover the many pleasures of reading and, hence, inspired my writing.

A Few Words from the Author

It's time to turn another page. No pun intended. In my last four books, my protagonist has been the fictitious British author of murder mysteries, Devon Stone. Suave and a lover of gin and tonics, dear Devon has perhaps gone on to other endeavors…but not in my books.

I have decided, however, to keep the same time frame in *this* book as in my previous mysteries. The early 1950s. I love the fact that we will be dealing, here, with *no* Internet, *no* cell phones, no CCTV. Actually the early 1950s saw the transition of CCTV from military to civilian use, although it was still primarily used in high-security areas.

Another challenge, of course, is bringing my 1950s characters to life for a 21st century audience with a whole different sense of values and morals.

My new protagonist in *A Perfect Murder Takes Time*, an author of best selling murder mysteries, is now an American-born one. Smart, inquisitive, a bit sarcastic at times, apprehensive and cautious at others, and always with the love of his life by his side.

Contrary to its title, however, this book *isn't* a thriller or whodunit as my others have been…but more like an historical fiction, a travelogue with a little philosophy and a couple of murders thrown in on the side for good measure. Actually, this is really just a long short story, as opposed to a full-length novel. The true definition of a novella. Not that I'm comparing myself in any way with Hemingway (wink, wink), but one of his great masterpieces, *The Old Man And The Sea*, was a novella, clocking in at a mere 26,531 words.

Mark Greaney, author of the thrilling *Gray Man* series, inspired the basic premise for *this* book. For pre-writing research, he and his wife travel to the various foreign lands that he intends to use in his next book. Sometimes accompanied by local guides, he wants the locales to be real, authentic, to be described in detail so that the reader gets a true sense of place.

Above all, pay attention to my words. Therefore, I encourage you to read my *Author's Notes* at the end of the story. Yes, you will learn a bit about Egypt: its history, its culture, and its people. Perhaps you will learn *more* than you bargained for. This book *may* arouse the ire in a few of my readers. It may ruffle some feathers and rattle some cages. Please don't take offense, as none was intended.

It's a cliché to say that travel is enlightening, but it's true. One never knows who or what their fellow travelers might be, what they have done, or what they *will* do. And they, in turn, don't know who or what *you* might be, or of what you might be capable.

So, sit back; perhaps grab some snacks, a cold beverage (adult or otherwise) and prepare to be enlightened, surprised, and, hopefully, totally engaged.

Fasten your seatbelts; we're ready for takeoff!

PART ONE

Thou Shalt Not...

Man's most valuable trait is a judicious sense of what not to believe.
Euripides

PROLOGUE

Cairo, Egypt – January 26, 1952...Black Saturday

No one knows, exactly, who really started the riots. It seemed to be a spontaneous anti-British protest that quickly escalated out of control. *Seriously* and violently out of control.

The British occupation of Egypt was now in its 70th year, although it was limited to the Suez Canal zone. Egypt had declared sovereignty in 1923, but the British government was still running interference. There had been several attacks against British forces in the area, which were being supported by Egyptian policemen. On January 25, 7,000 British troops surrounded an Egyptian police station in Ismailia, which had been harboring the group that had fired on the British forces. A gunshot was fired from inside the police station, which initiated a fierce firefight. The British suffered minor casualties, but fifty Egyptian police officers were killed and eighty wounded. The British forces took the surviving police officers into captivity at that time.

When news of this confrontation reached Cairo the next day, the Egyptian public became irate. For some reason then, the unrest began at Almaza Airport when workers refused to service British Airplanes. That was followed by a police demonstration at a barracks, followed even further by the protesters being joined by students at the Cairo University buildings. Together the large (and growing larger) group marched toward the Prime Minister's office to demand that Egypt break its diplomatic relations with the United Kingdom and declare war on Britain. Needless to say, that faced opposition from King Farouk I. Then the protesters were enraged not only by the British, but also by the Egyptian king and his supporters. Ultimately chaos ensued.

The first act of arson was the burning of the Casino Opera, an entertainment club. Unfortunately the fire rapidly spread out of control to surrounding buildings…a hotel, an automobile club, a bank, and several other shops, offices, and movie theaters.

The horrendous conflagration, which had started shortly after noontime, ended at 11:00 that night.

Nearly three-hundred shops had been destroyed, including some of Egypt's most famous department stores, thirty corporate offices, thirteen hotels, forty movie theaters, over seventy coffeehouses, restaurants and social clubs.

Aside from the enormous catastrophic destruction of property, twenty-six people died and five hundred fifty-two suffered injuries such as burns and bone fractures.

Egyptian Army troops quickly moved in to restore order of some sort, but the instability and lack of public confidence would pave the way for a larger and more violent revolution in the coming months.

Overlooked, however, when Cairo was trying to clean up the mess from the chaotic melee, and totally unrelated to the political unrest, was one very blatant and nasty murder.

1

Two and a half weeks earlier
New York City - 5:30 P.M.

Running from 53rd to 59th Streets between First Avenue and the East River, Sutton Place serves as the gateway to the fashionable Upper East Side. It was one of the most expensive places in the city in which to live. Power brokers and celebrities of all types called this place home. Number 220 Sutton Place South, a glorious old building, had two elevator banks and four doormen who knew every tenant's names, including those of their beloved pets.

Marcus Darke, in his tenth floor apartment at 220, stood at his living room window overlooking the East River. The cold, torrential rain had slowed traffic across the Queensboro Bridge to a crawl as commuters inched their ways home through the darkening early evening. Bumper-to-bumper headlights heading in one direction, nothing but brake lights going in the other. If it hadn't been for its running lights, an old tugboat pushing a long barge filled with garbage would have floated unnoticed as it passed under the bridge.

Poor suckers, Marcus Darke thought to himself as he watched the traffic on the bridge. *I can't imagine doing that every single day. It would drive me bonkers. Bonkers in Yonkers.*

He had probably never even been to Yonkers. He just liked the sound of it.

Marcus Darke was the young author of a four-book series of extremely popular murder mysteries. His loyal fans eagerly awaited each new publication, always with the familiar tag line under the title: ANOTHER

DARKE MYSTERY. He published his first book at the age of twenty-nine and now, at thirty-five, he was just about to begin his latest. Each book was set in some distant, foreign locale, with nefarious characters of both genders and multiple races. Some of his astute readers may have picked up that the locales he selects, starting with book one, are in alphabetical order. The first book was set in Austria, the second in Belgium, the next in Cyprus, and the latest violent best seller had been set in the icy chill of wintry Denmark. His very first book, *Dancing With The Devil*, took the publishing world by storm and by surprise, staying on the New York Times Bestseller List for seventy-five weeks. It was soon purchased by Hollywood and then turned into one of the highest-grossing films of 1948. Hence the luxurious, lavishly furnished, art-filled eight-room apartment overlooking the borough of Queens.

His wife, Valencia, had been a history major at Cornell where they met. Marcus, an English Lit major, worked on *The Cornell Daily Sun*, an independent student-run newspaper where he honed his writing skills. He fell in love with Valencia almost at first sight. Married, now, for ten years she is his main resource for all the research material that is necessary for his intricately written, detail filled murder mysteries.

Valencia was his voice of reason. Marcus could be flighty. Valencia was logical. Marcus was impulsive. It proved to be a good, sensible combination and they rarely argued.

Marcus Darke caught sight of movement behind him reflected in the window. He slowly turned to face his wife as she approached with two martinis in hand.

"Our passports were *finally* returned today", she said, handing him a glass, "with the required visas for our trip."

"Wonderful," he replied with a huge smile and raising his glass as in a toast. "Just in time. That was too close for comfort. I was getting concerned. Here's to us, Val. This should be an exciting trip. At least in a warmer, drier climate than we've been experiencing lately. I'm *really* looking forward to this one."

Valencia smiled, shaking her head.

"I still can't get used to that silly little mustache you're attempting to grow. Trying to look like Clark Gable?"

"Not at all," Marcus laughed, as he ran a finger across the stubbly growth under his nose. "Just trying to make this baby face of mine look a tad older. And maybe a bit more sophisticated."

Throwing his head back, he struck a pose.

Giggling, she wrinkled up her nose.

"Silly! You might want to rethink it. It doesn't appear in your passport photo. Then again, maybe it won't matter. Frankly, Marcus, I think you should lose it."

They clinked their glasses together and sipped their drinks.

"I'm sure, Marcus, that you have something in mind with this new book but...well, I'm fairly certain that Agatha Christie already covered this territory that we're going to pretty well."

"Yes, she did that *very* well. And, yes, my publisher had the exact same comments. But I'm thinking of taking a different direction. Very different. I have already begun with some thoughts and some notes. I've been keeping up with the news and I feel certain that some political unrest is afoot over there. Perhaps some political intrigue is just ripe for a good murder or two among the tombs and temples."

Marcus Darke worked for approximately eight or nine months writing each one of his books. He'd be secluded away in front of his typewriter, laughing at times, cringing at others, referring to his notes and calling upon his imagination. Doing location research prior to beginning his writing, he and Valencia would spend time exploring the country in which each one of the mysteries would be set. They took notes and roll after roll of film. Valencia's camera was constantly by her side. He wanted actual locales. Real places. He liked detail. And he liked accuracy. And his fans loved his humor along with the murder and mayhem. Half the fun of the writing was doing the extensive research beforehand. Despite his sometimes-violent fictional crimes, Marcus had never actually been associated in any way with a *real* murderer.

That would soon change.

A few weeks earlier, Marcus had wired a twenty-five percent advance into the account of the guide he had commissioned for this trip. Marcus had told the guide, via telegram, that he wanted this trip to be totally first class and to spare no expense when the itinerary was put together. Most of *his* exploratory traveling expenses would be a tax write-off because he being an author constituted as a business. Much to Valencia's chagrin, Marcus had invited his best friend, Sebastian Reckling, to accompany them on the trip. Obviously the expenses for Valencia and Sebastian would *not* be deductible. That didn't concern him at all, even though the total cost that he had been quoted was staggering.

He had no way of anticipating, however, how the guide would change his life forever, or the adventure that lay ahead.

New York City - 11:05 P.M.

Sebastian Reckling leaned back in the big leather chair behind his desk and let out a sigh. He glanced at his watch. He hadn't realized how many hours had passed since he arrived at his office shortly before three that afternoon. He closed and pushed aside his favorite and oft-read book: *On The Witness Stand.* The German-American psychologist Hugo Munsterberg wrote it in 1915. This was the book that had gotten him interested in psychology, more specifically leading into forensic psychology and later, even *more* interestingly, forensic linguistics. In other words, through mere observation, listening to what was being said, not said, and body language, he had the uncanny and unfailing ability to tell when someone was lying. It served him well.

He had been classmates and eventually becoming good friends with Marcus Darke at Cornell. It was there that Sebastian had earned the nickname of "Reckless" because of his careless driving habits, excessive drinking, and lustful dating…often multiple girls in the same evening.

Twice married and twice divorced, childless in both cases, he continued the reckless habit of dating and abandoning beautiful young females. Now nearly thirty-six years old, he was tall and strikingly handsome, with sandy blond hair and limpid blue eyes that seemed to intensify when he drank his favored bourbon on the rocks.

Aside from this, he was often called upon by his friend Marcus when the author needed some input regarding developing his nefarious characters, or in discussing the psychological motivation behind their evil and murderous deeds.

In need of a long overdue vacation, a month earlier he was therefore extremely surprised and delighted when he had received an invitation to accompany Marcus and his wife on their trip abroad. The thought of a new adventure in a mysterious culture intrigued him greatly and he accepted without hesitation.

Regarding his successful freelance career, Sebastian was given small office spaces in a few of Manhattan's top law firms to be utilized when he was hired on for analyzing current cases as a consultant and advisor. Working for both defending and prosecuting attorneys, he had been successful for years in assuring guilty or not guilty verdicts in notorious crimes, primarily of murder.

At the moment, he was currently sitting in such an office at Bird & Drake, a prestigious legal office at 370 Lexington Avenue. Even though it was close to Grand Central Terminal, it would be almost impossible for him to catch the 11:39 train to his home in New Rochelle.

"Shit!" he exclaimed out loud, rubbing his sleepy eyes.

The rain that had been falling earlier in the evening apparently had stopped and, as he glanced out of the window, many of the surrounding office buildings were now dark and the traffic down below on the streets was sparse.

A light tapping on his door startled him. It opened slowly and cautiously.

"I hope I didn't startle you," said Calista Faircloth with a little chuckle. "I knew you were still here because I saw the light under the door."

"I didn't know anyone else was still here in the offices aside from security," Sebastian answered with a large smile across his face. "What the hell kept *you* here so late?"

"I know you've seen that mock-up courtroom downstairs. We were rehearsing the opening statement with one of our newer lawyers. The murder case he's handling goes to trial tomorrow. Well, mere hours away now. I was impressed. He's going to be a real rock star."

Calista Faircloth, a tall, raven-haired beautiful woman of twenty-eight, was a paralegal well-respected for her talents by everyone in the firm.

"Ironically," she continued, "it's somewhat similar to that Lawford case that we worked on with you last year, although this time there is no question about the perpetrator's guilt."

Todd Lawford, scion of the Lawford family...the Lawfords of Scarsdale, was the estranged son of a wealthy financial advisor who had been accused of violently killing his pregnant girlfriend while he was drunk. Despite glaring evidence to the contrary, an intuitive Sebastian

Reckling was convinced via his many interviews with the accused that the young man was innocent. It was a shocking case that generated front-page coverage in the New York press where the accused was vilified practically daily. The financial advisor and his wife were high society and their son was an embarrassment. The trial seemed to drag on for weeks and when the verdict of not guilty was finally announced there were audible gasps from the spectators and pronouncements from the press that the trial had been mishandled, the jury was tainted, and the man had gotten away with murder. Literally.

Unbeknownst to the press however, as the trial had been proceeding, Sebastian Reckling had sought interviews with the accused man's estranged parents. They were very forthcoming in their eagerness to see that their son received the harshest of punishments. As a matter of fact, they were *so* forthcoming, and Sebastian was so attuned to speech patterns, what people were saying (or not saying), and body language, he was able to deduce without question that the accused man's mother had been the one to actually commit the crime.

"Look, it's really late," Calista said with a wide smile, glancing at her watch, "As you well know, I live just two stops uptown on the IRT. Gather your files and that big book of yours and come on. Why not crash at my place tonight and forget about your train on the New Haven Line?"

Sebastian Reckling shrugged his shoulders and winked. This was not the first time such an invitation had been given and accepted. "Well, if you insist," he said with a wink.

They both chuckled as he stood up to go, gathering his files as he did so. He turned out the lights in his office and closed the door behind him as they walked down the hall toward the elevators.

"How about a sneak preview, my dear?" he said to Calista.

She quickly glanced around to make sure that, indeed, they were the only ones on this floor at this late hour.

They were still kissing passionately when the elevator dinged and the doors opened revealing, fortunately, an empty car.

Calista Faircloth knew his "Reckless" reputation and, in return, Sebastian Reckling knew *hers*. She was smart. She was beyond beautiful. And she knew how to satisfy handsome young men, especially when they both were naked. They each played the field and were experts in their game.

But the one thing that Calista *didn't* know was that Sebastian, even with all of his womanizing, still carried the proverbial torch for what he thought was the love of his life. The woman he still craved deeply. The score that he *must* eventually make. Somehow. Someway. That special woman he met at Cornell. The young, beautiful, enchanting Valencia Roberts...now Valencia Darke, his best friend's wife.

2

As typical for this time of year, the sky was overcast as it had been for the past two weeks. The chance of precipitation was low and the anticipation of an upcoming trip abroad was high within the Carter household. Adeline and her twin brother Adam had resided together practically since birth, eighty years ago. They doted on one another and were rarely far apart. They were a familiar sight when they were hustling about the various shops in town and they had the reputation for being a lovable, sweet, if sometimes befuddled old couple.

White-haired Adeline was somewhat plump with a wagging wattle under her chin that was rapidly in motion whenever she spoke. Her mind was razor-sharp, and she enjoyed a good joke and tall tales now and then, but it was never in poor taste. Her stories always kept her rapt audiences in stitches with her wry humor and sarcasm. She also enjoyed a small glass of gin every afternoon at four when they were at home and not traveling.

Adam, older by ten minutes but looking younger by ten years, was more reserved but seemed to constantly have a twinkle in his eye. He was the one to plan their various trips to foreign lands, which they did so sometimes more than once a year. Adam did extensive research via correspondences with the Fleet Street offices of Thomas Cook & Son, organizers of unique, specialized tours, and had itineraries plotted out weeks before their departure. Every afternoon at four he enjoyed a shot or two of good Irish whiskey.

"You have a spot of egg on your chin, dear," Adeline said to Adam as they sat at the breakfast table. She motioned with her finger to the exact spot on her own chin for reference. "Listen to that, will you? The blasted wind is picking up again. That old kitchen window is rattling. I shall be glad to get to warmer climates in a few days when we're on holiday. The older I get, the more I despise winter. Makes my bones ache. I suppose that's typical, though. Bah! I'm becoming a doddering old biddy, aren't I, dear?"

"Oh, no, Addy. Not you. But I agree about the cold. Let's clean up here. We must go into town. I had requested that the bank get the foreign exchange monies that we'll need. They promised that it would be there this morning."

No one in town ever questioned where or how this sweet old couple got their money, they only knew that the Carters, despite their occasional travels and quiet, seemingly conservative lifestyle, apparently must be extremely wealthy.

The Carters *were*, indeed, extremely wealthy and had been for decades. They were also extremely lucky and had been for decades. Not once ever being caught or even suspected, the Carters were adroit liars, pickpockets, thieves…and cold-blooded murderers.

Cairo, Egypt - 10:45 A.M.

Baako (pronounced Bah-koh) Mustafa made his way through the crowded and noisy corridors of the labyrinthian Khan el-Khalili bazaar. The handsome young Egyptologist was a popular and well-known persona throughout not only the city but also basically the entire country. At twenty-seven, he had unusually chiseled good looks, and squared facial features, not typical of most Egyptian men. Dark, wavy hair and brown – almost black–eyes, framed by the kind of eyelashes a woman would kill for. Young women found him enticing and would often brazenly flirt with him. He found it amusing and flattering, but he was far more interested in learning as much as he could about his ancient ancestors than finding female companionship. Yes, he wanted a family, but love could wait a while. He was not in any hurry. And, frankly, no woman had intrigued him enough to pursue any type of friendship, let alone romance. Egyptian men usually lived with their parents until they wed but, with his parents deceased, both lost to typhoid, he now resided alone in their apartment in Agouza, one of the nine municipal districts that form Giza city, a part of greater Cairo. He loved and missed them greatly and sometimes he still felt their presence among the rooms.

Khan el-Khalili, one of Cairo's main attractions for tourists and Egyptians alike, is occupied by countless dozens of local merchants and traders significantly geared toward the tourist trade, selling souvenirs, antiques, and jewelry. Most of it is, in reality, junk. But it sells. In addition to the shops, there are several maqha (coffeehouses), restaurants and street food vendors. In other words, the place is very aromatic almost constantly. Spice markets added to the color and fragrances. One such market was Baako's destination this morning. He enjoyed cooking and was in need of more cumin and cardamom, favored spices in Egyptian cooking.

Several vendors called out to him as he walked down the alleyways.

"Sabah alkhayr, Baako!"

"Hey, Baako! Sabah al kheir!"

He would wave and call greetings back to them in return.

Before arriving at his usual spice market, a friend called out to him from an outdoor table at a popular morning spot, El Fishawy's. It was one of the oldest and most famous coffeehouses in the bazaar, having been established in 1773.

"Ahlaan, Baako, sit with me, please," his friend said as he motioned for the young man to join him, and then inhaled on his hooka.

"Sabah alkhayr, Hossam," Baako responded as he took a seat next to the old man. "I trust you are well?"

Hossam Mahfouz, a grizzled man in his late seventies, exhaling smoke smelling of tobacco and mint, shrugged his shoulders, nodded his head and threw up his hands in a questioning gesture.

"What can I say, eh, Baako? The sun shines on my face this morning. Seeing another dawn always gives me hope for the day."

And the two men laughed.

A server wearing a dusty old blue and white striped galabiya and a white turban brought a brass tray carrying two glasses of hot Koshary tea brewed with cane sugar and fresh mint leaves. He bowed slightly to Baako and set them down on the small table.

"Perhaps you have heard, my young friend," Hossam Mahfouz began as he raised a glass of tea, "the rumblings of discontent that I have heard. I fear much danger ahead for us."

"Yes, I, too, have heard such distressing rumblings. God's willing, that's all they will remain. Just rumblings and no violence."

Again, the old man shrugged his shoulders.

"An American author, his wife, and a good friend of theirs are arriving in a few days," Baako continued, taking a sip from his tea. "He will be doing research for his next book and has commissioned me to be their personal guide for two weeks. I intend to give them an adventure they'll never forget. I truly hope it will be a *safe* one."

"Ah, Baako," the old man replied loudly, "no one could have a better guide than you, my young friend. Your knowledge of our glorious history astounds even *me*...and I've been around since our last pharaoh, Cleopatra."

A couple of the patrons at the surrounding tables laughed at that one.

"After he contacted me I *did* read his books. They are murder mysteries. Something I normally would not read. But they are very good. Very clever. Obviously well researched. He must be planning to write about scoundrels with evil deeds lurking around our city or our desert. Or along the Nile."

Hossam Mahfouz closed his eyes and shook his head.

"God's willing, he won't stir up any of our Djinn, my young friend. I fear that in these troubling times they would be too eager to take vengeance on rabble-rousers, Egyptian or otherwise. Written or otherwise."

In Arabic mythology, Djinn are powerful, unseen demons or spirits with the ability to take on various forms, human or animal, and can dwell in such inanimate objects such as stones, trees, ruins and underneath the earth, in the air, and in fire. The Quran describes Djinn as spirits made from smokeless fire and were created before humans. They can be both feared and admired, as they can be benevolent as well as destructive and deadly.

"Remember," the old man continued, wagging his index finger for emphasis, "the Djinn will have no power over anyone who arms himself with God's verses."

Baako nodded and smiled politely, concealing his disbelief in these mythical manifestations. The older generations still believed in such things. The younger generation, not so much.

The old man offered his water pipe to Baako who politely declined.

"I am grateful for your warning, my friend," Baako said as he finished his tea and stood up to leave, tossing a few coins on the table for the server. "Now I must hasten to see Hajj al-Bayumi for my spices down the next alleyway and then my horses need their morning grooming and workout."

"Ah, yes, Baako. I remember your beautiful creatures. Are you riding today?"

"I have a sunset ride into the Western Desert and around the pyramids scheduled for this evening with some tourists from Germany. Hopefully they won't spook my beauties."

"I have watched you, my friend, riding your magnificent steed across the sands. Black as ebony, he is. Glistening in the sun."

"My beloved Khufu. We ride as one. We race our own shadows."

"Better be faster than the shadows of the Djinn!" Hossam Mahfouz called out.

Baako laughed, shaking his head, and waved goodbye as he disappeared down a crowded alleyway.

His smile dissipated before he had taken three steps. His old friend's concern about the increasing unrest in the streets had not gone unheeded and was not unexpected. Egypt had long sought its freedom from British colonial rule. Baako felt that the time was fast approaching for a revolution of sorts. But perpetrated by whom and when? While initially popular, Egypt's King Farouk's reputation was rapidly eroding due to the corruption and incompetence of his government. Ascending to the throne when he was only sixteen, he was more interested in his own extravagant playboy lifestyle than governing with reason and maturity.

Baako Mustafa was concerned about what lay ahead for his beloved country. He was also concerned about the safety of the travelers from abroad who would be arriving later in the week.

3

The storm of the night before had passed and the sun shone brightly into the east-facing windows of the Darke apartment. In his small office, Marcus, with his upper lip now cleanly shaved, was at his typewriter with words flowing like the waters down the East River rushing out to sea. Valencia sat in a comfortable chair next to his desk sipping her second cup of coffee for the morning. Marcus was on his third. She was reading the New York Herald Tribune, once regarded as a "writer's newspaper".

"As well as you know me, you probably must have suspected that this has been brewing in the back of my mind for weeks. For the life of me, Marcus," she said, letting out a rather loud sigh and putting the newspaper down after moments of silence. "I have no idea *why* you would *ever* invite Reckless to join us on this trip. I wish you had asked me first. You've not done that before and I know *you* know that he has had a crush on me since our Cornell days. He's made it painfully obvious at inopportune times. Well, to *me* anyway. I sincerely hope that he doesn't make this trip uncomfortable."

"I know, dear," answered Marcus nonchalantly as he kept typing without looking up. "I've thought about this for a while. And, yes, I know he has had the hots for you. I'm *not* naive. Certainly he's been less than subtle. Don't worry. We haven't called him Reckless for nothing. He loves challenges. Always has. So I plan on giving him quite a challenge. I'm going to race him up to the top of one of the pyramids...and push him off."

Valencia Darke simply stared at her husband, mouth agape.

300 E. 61st Street, NYC - 8:30 A.M.

Calista Faircloth was neatly dressed and ready to head off to her office. She stood at her bathroom mirror applying her lipstick as Sebastian Reckling was behind her, in the shower. She smiled and turned, pulling back the shower curtain. His well-toned and dripping body didn't react. He simply put a bar of soap back in its dish, and just stood there with his hands on his hips as the water beat down on him.

"You're steaming up my mirror," she said with a smirk.

"Am I steaming *you* up as well?" Sebastian asked as he swiveled his hips from side to side.

Calista laughed heartily.

"Oh, you did a splendid job of that last night, you bad boy."

Sebastian turned off the shower and Calista handed him a towel as he stepped from the tub out onto the small bathroom rug.

"I've got to run. Stay as long as you need, handsome. There's still some coffee left in the pot in the kitchen. Just remember to pull the front door closed behind you when you leave. It will lock."

She leaned in, giving him a soft kiss on his cheek. Then she reached down and very gently squeezed his balls.

"Keep those boys safe on your trip," she said, glancing down. "I hope to see them again when you get back home."

"Get that silly look off your face, Val," Marcus Darke laughed as he pushed back from his typewriter. "You *must* know I was only joking about that. Wouldn't surprise me a bit, though, if he tried to push *me* off that pyramid...if we even *do* get the chance to climb one."

"For such an acclaimed psychologist," Valencia said shaking her head, "he's pretty lousy with relationships. I thought his first two wives were simply lovely. And he cheated on them both. It's *him* that's the problem."

"He's been a big help to me with some of my characters and story lines. I'd consider him a good friend, but..."

"But why, then, would you ever invite him to travel halfway around the globe with us. For the sake of a good book? Sure, he's a smart man and good at what he does but, nevertheless, I'm a bit apprehensive, Marcus."

"I have my reasons, Val. That's all. Don't worry. Yes, it was very improper and impolite not to ask you first. Too late, I know, but I apologize for my inconsideration."

In actuality, Marcus Darke had acted on sheer impulse, with no real reason in mind. He and his friend were on the telephone discussing the upcoming trip and, without giving it a second thought, Marcus had simply blurted out an invitation. He never expected Reckless to accept. But a card laid is a card played. It was a done deal, and that was that. He was too embarrassed to tell Valencia that he had no reasons in mind.

Sebastian Reckling, on the other hand, may have had some reasons for accepting the unexpected invitation so readily.

"Look, we'll have a fabulous trip, Val. The Egyptologist that I've commissioned as our guide has an outstanding reputation. It will be fun. It will be educational. And it *will* be exciting. The experience will surely lead to yet another best-selling Darke Mystery…that is, if we don't all succumb to the dreaded curse of the mummy."

Marcus Darke laughed. Valencia Darke did not.

In the not too distant past, she had always found his wisecracks —as crisp as rifle shots at dawn—funny. Not so with this one.

Sebastian Reckling toweled off and left the bathroom, dropping his wet towel into a hamper that was behind the door. He then slowly padded, naked, out to the kitchen to get a cup of coffee. It was just lukewarm, but he didn't care. Leaning up against the counter as he drank, he scanned the headlines of the morning paper. Nothing grabbed his attention, so he downed his coffee, rinsed out the cup and replaced it in the cupboard.

He meandered back into the bedroom where he saw his clothes, thrown off in lustful haste the evening before, scattered around on the floor. He bent down to pick up his trousers and saw a pair of men's underwear that had apparently been either kicked or thrown under the bed. They weren't his.

He chuckled as he continued dressing. *Obviously some poor sap left here commando style*, he thought to himself. *Wonder if they belong to that new rock star lawyer?*

"Did she say rock star or rock hard?" He chuckled to himself out loud.

Fifteen minutes later he was on the subway heading back downtown to Grand Central Terminal where he then caught the first train up to New Rochelle and home.

Soon his life would change in a most unexpected way.

Marcus Darke put down the newspaper he had been reading after Valencia had finished with it.

"Hey, sweet pea," he said with a smile. "How about a movie tonight? *The Greatest Show On Earth* is playing at Radio City. That and the Rockettes might help assuage your apprehensions. I'll even spring for dinner at the Rainbow Room just across the street. I know you love that place."

Valencia couldn't help but laugh.

"You are such a smooth talker, you are. You know just the right thing to say at just the right time. You're right, though. I am probably being just foolish for no reason. Sure, sure, sure, let's go tonight. Oh, wait. Don't you want to call Reckless and invite *him*, too? We can all hold hands in the movie theater."

Marcus leaned back and let out a loud hoot.

"Valencia, you are the best. I love it when you speak sarcasm to me! Turns me on, for sure."

Valencia swatted him away with the flick of her wrist.

Soon their lives would change in a most unexpected way.

4

Baako Mustafa had been interested in his country's history and culture for as long as he could remember. He was an inquisitive, exceptional student in school and eventually got his higher education at King Fuad I University. Its main campus was in Giza, immediately across the Nile from Cairo, practically in the shadows of the Great Pyramids. To become a good Egyptologist he had to become proficient in English, French and German, as well as his own native Arabic, obviously. He continued his studies and soon earned the required PHD to become an Egyptologist.

He graduated with honors and was extremely popular among his peers. Even with his impressive credentials, however, there was only one job available for every five trained Egyptologists. He longed to do fieldwork or eventually become a curator in the prestigious Cairo Museum. He just had to be patient.

But then Fate stepped in. With his educational reputation, good looks, command of four languages, and enchanting personality he was called upon by several tour groups to become a guide, which he did so gladly, earning quite a respectable living. He quickly became known from Alexandria on the Mediterranean all the way down to Abu Simbel in the south. It was because of this reputation that he was sought after and commissioned, on occasion, by wealthy tourists to be their personal, independent guide, shunning the larger tour groups. This is where he *really* earned exceptionally good money. He could set whatever daily rate he wished and it was never disputed. Never haggled over.

Consequently, he was booked solid practically every week in one capacity or the other. And, even at his young age, he was quickly becoming a very wealthy Egyptian.

He owned and had trained three beautiful Baladi horses, a breed native to Egypt, different from the better-known Egyptian Arabian. The name, Baladi, actually means "horse of the country". He boarded them at the exclusive Pharaoh's Riding Academy, a stone's throw from the Great Pyramids. His horses were very well tended to by eager, attentive young grooms when he traveled away as a tour guide.

He knew about his country and culture. He knew about horses. He knew about the unrest that was bubbling almost to the boiling point. But the one thing that he *didn't* know was that his life was soon to change in a most unexpected way.

Adeline Carter and her brother Adam, both nicknamed Addy, hustled about in preparation for their trip. Every once in a while, as he was passing the front windows, Adam would glance toward the little cottage across Wendling Road, their small country lane. An early morning fog had dissipated.

"Strange, Addy," he said pulling back the drapery. "I haven't noticed that old busybody Eudora Smythe out and about lately. She usually heads off to the markets a couple times each week. I've seen her drive out and then back. She concerned me, she did. Asking too many prodding questions about us. I found her impudent and rude, didn't you?"

"Oh, I did indeed, dear. I, too, was concerned about her annoying prodding. Made me quite uneasy at times with her insinuating remarks. She said something last week that took me aback. Something possibly quite damaging. So, I simply had to take matters into my own hands. Yes, I did. Just that. Sorry that I forgot to mention it to you, dear. Just slipped my old mind, it did. I paid that poor, lonely, and much too nosey widow a courteous little visit a couple days ago. Surprised her with my friendliness and generosity. I baked her one of my delicious loaves of nut bread. She invited me in and offered me some tea and a slice but I declined. I hope she enjoyed it…rest her soul."

Placing her tongue in cheek.

Adam Carter let out a loud laugh clapping his hands together.

"One of your usual *special* ingredients, I have no doubt?"

Adeline cackled like an old witch and answered with a broad smile and a wink.

"It pays to read Agatha Christie, doesn't it? She's the expert on such things. Thallium is most effective, dear. Most effective. I'm surprised that no one else has missed her yet. Obviously there's been no police or ambulance on the scene so far. You would have noticed *that*, dear, wouldn't you have? One of the downfalls, I suppose, of being a crotchety old bitch that no one seems to care about. Pity."

Her brother simply shrugged his shoulders and turned away from the window.

"I called the airlines this morning to reconfirm our flights," Adam said nonchalantly without giving his neighbor a second thought.

"Well, done, Addy," Adeline responded. "I never dread any of our flights, no matter how long. They're usually a pleasure. I just dread the long uncomfortable train rides to and from Gatwick. Oh, perhaps you should call old Thomas Cook while you're at it to thank him for putting together such a wonderful itinerary," she said with another wink and a broad smile.

"I'm afraid," Adam replied with a laugh, "that would be a *very* long distance call, wouldn't it? To either Heaven or Hell…wherever the old boy might be. You're assuming, at this point, that our holiday *will* be wonderful."

And they both laughed.

"Oh, it shall be, really," Adeline responded.

"I shall put the kettle on for some tea, Addy," said Adam. "Shall I also make us some sandwiches for lunch?"

"No, thank you, dear. I am going to prepare us a nice Shepard's Pie for our evening meal. Tea and scones will suffice for lunch as far as I'm concerned."

The topic of the recent and, as of yet, undiscovered demise of their neighbor never came up in conversation again. They simply went on about their business. As usual. With more than a dozen unsolved murders in their wake.

The twins, Adeline and Adam Carter, were born in January of 1872. Ironically, considering what they have become, the very same month that the trial began for Christiana Edmunds, the Brighton "Chocolate

Cream Killer". She had purchased confectionary from a local shop, laced the sweets with strychnine and returned them to the shop to be sold to the unsuspecting public. She had purchased the strychnine from a local chemist on the pretense that she needed to poison some pesky feral cats that were annoying her neighborhood. She increased her poisoning endeavors by sending parcels of the tainted chocolates to prominent persons, even sending parcels to *herself* claiming that she, too, was a victim of the poisoner. She was eventually found out, tried, convicted, and spent the remainder of her years at the Broadmoor Criminal Lunatic Asylum.

By the time the Carter twins were in their early teens they read about this heinous crime that had occurred years before and became intrigued. And influenced.

Despite her jovial personality and genuine wit, Adeline left her teenage years behind without any young male ever asking her out on a date. Adam showed no interest in girls whatsoever. Nor boys, for that matter.

Their mother doted on them and loved them dearly. Their father, a wealthy banker and financier, was aloof, to say the least. They couldn't remember him even once giving them a loving hug, a kiss, or a word of endearment.

Having read and thoroughly enjoying, *Oliver Twist*, Adam was influenced and tried his hand at picking pockets. Carefully, at first. More aggressive and successful as the years went by. Their father was constantly confused by the fact that he thought he had much more money in his wallet than he actually found at times.

When they were twenty-two, still unwed and living at home, their mother, already a frail woman, succumbed to influenza. Their father, inconsolable, then became more verbally abusive to the twins.

"Jesus Christ!" he drunkenly raved one evening a month after his wife had been buried...and two days before Christmas. "I guess now I'm stuck with *you* two here living with me for the rest of my bloody life. A fat cow and a fairy. What a pair! Joy to the fucking world!"

Adeline seethed and Adam cried.

But then Adeline took matters into her own hands. Yes, she did. Just that.

The next night she slipped a little something extra into the Baccarat brandy decanter from which her father poured his drink every evening after dinner, thereby causing cardiac arrest. The twins stood back and watched to make sure their father was actually dead before calling for medical assistance.

Unbeknownst to one another, a few of the mourners following the man's funeral five days later discovered upon arriving home that some items they thought they had on their person when the funeral began were now gone.

A gold pocket watch.

"Blast," said its wealthy owner, "how bloody clumsy of me. Must have slipped out of my vest."

An elegant diamond bracelet that was worth thousands.

"Mercy," cried its white-haired owner now in tears and nearly fainting, "that old clasp must have broken!"

A sterling silver Waldmann fountain pen.

"Shite!" exclaimed the banker who had owned it. "I was positive I had it in my breast pocket. Perhaps not."

Adam Carter had enjoyed all those consoling hugs in more ways than one.

The twins, therefore, inherited the large house that was old before they were born and which had long since been paid for, along with all of their father's substantial financial wealth. Adam Carter then became quite adept at continuing their father's investment opportunities in the stock market. Throughout the following decades what had been a small fortune became a large one.

Adeline and Adam traveled the globe throughout all those years and always returned home with a profit: money and jewelry having been lifted from unsuspecting fellow travelers.

They were soon to affect the lives of several *others* in various and unexpected ways.

5

Meanwhile in Giza, Egypt...

The Mena House, built in 1869, was initially a hunting lodge, nicknamed the "Mud Hut". It was owned by 'Ismail the Magnificent, the Khedive of Egypt. Due to some unpleasant political matters, he sold the place to a married couple for their private residence. They expanded it and then sold it once again to an English couple. They continued the expansion and then opened it in 1886 as the Mena House Hotel. It was named after the founding father of the first Egyptian dynasty, Mena (or King) Menes. The hotel was utilized as a hospital for Australian soldiers during the Great War...World War I.

Because of its sumptuous renovations and prime locale...practically right across the street and over a sandy strip of the Western Desert from the Great Pyramids...the Mena House became *the* place to stay in the Cairo area. Such luminaries as Charlie Chaplin, Frank Sinatra, Sarah Bernhardt were guests and Sir Arthur Conan Doyle spent an entire season as an honored guest. One of the earlier owners of the Mena House pioneered the employment of female staff in the hotel. He had tour-operators conduct a house-to-house survey to find out which women had graduated from college, but were now sitting at home and wasting their degrees. Many of these women were then offered jobs. He insisted on having personable young women working in his hotels.

One of these fortunate and personable young ladies was Manal Khalifa. At twenty-seven, she was a striking beauty. Long wavy raven hair, smooth skin the color of coffee with a lot of cream, sparkling black eyes that looked like onyx marbles, eyelids accented with kohl, and a lilting voice coming from a mouth that almost always had a smile. One didn't need to push their imagination too far to see that she resembled the famous bust of Nefertiti. Manal had received her BA and PhD. degrees in Tourism and Egyptology from the Faculty of Tourism and Hotel Management in Cairo. She had become proficient in speaking excellent English, almost perfect French, and spoke enough German to wish someone "good health" when they might sneeze. Those languages were needed to become an Egyptologist, although, at this point, she wasn't sure if she really wanted to do any fieldwork. It was her enticing personality that had won the hearts of those who interviewed her at the Mena House. At first, she had been hired as an assistant in the small office in the hotel that arranged tours for the guests. Just recently she had been promoted to manager when the former manager accepted a similar position at the Winter Palace in Luxor. Manal worked very professionally with other outside tour companies that had selected the Mena House as the place to stay for their clients, as well as setting up tours for such guests who wanted independent travel. On her two days off during the week, she often took a few of the hotel guests to the huge old Cairo Museum and expounded on the history that she knew so well. Never getting tired of seeing it, she always stood in awe staring at the golden funerary mask of Tutankhamun, which was encased in a large glass cube. The young king's tomb had been discovered in the Valley of the Kings in1922 by the British archaeologist Howard Carter and hundreds of the treasures from his tomb were on proud display in the museum.

Aside from her winning personality, Manal possessed a strong will. A *very* strong will. A bit unusual for young Egyptian women. Unmarried, she lived at home with her parents who had tried to arrange a marriage for her more than once since she turned eighteen. She thwarted the attempts and spurned her suitors, which frustrated her parents, especially her equally strong-willed father. Manal's two older sisters were long since wed and produced grandchildren for their parents to gloat over. Her older brother, Aharon, had a wife pregnant with their third child and, known only to Manal, he maintained three Christian mistresses on the side. Egyptian law actually allowed a man to have up to four *wives* at once, but having mistresses who were Christian, not Muslim, was another matter entirely. It could spell trouble. A nuisance the man did not want. Her brother had no qualms about threatening her with bodily harm if she ever told anyone and, like an obedient, albeit judging sister, she remained silent.

But her life was about to change in an unexpected way.

Once again, Baako Mustafa was walking the alleyways in the Khan el-Khalili bazaar. He stopped in his tracks when he saw his old friend, Hossam Mahfouz, approaching with an overwhelming bouquet of flowers. Baako was taken aback by the man's appearance. He was cleanly shaven, was wearing what appeared to be a brand new red galabiya, a burgundy fez, and the largest smile Baako could ever remember being on his friend's face.

"Masa' al-khair, my friend", Baako said with an equally warm smile. "I hesitate to ask, are you going to a wedding or a funeral?"

The old man laughed until tears were in his eyes.

"Here I am, Baako, a gentleman of seventy-eight, and I am about to marry for the very first time!"

Baako stood with his mouth agape.

"What motivated you, sir, passion or senility?"

The old man drew his head back like a cat that sees a dog approaching and laughed once again.

"Ah, dear boy, at my age passion takes time to be aroused. Senility has been knocking on my door for years and I have unanswered it. My sweet young bride, a widow for this past year, has a beauty and many attributes like no other."

"Exactly *how* young, Hossam?"

"She will soon turn seventy."

Baako snickered.

"And *many* attributes, you say? A widow. Hmmm...would money be one of those attributes?"

"Well...that, too," Hossam answered with a shrug.

Baako rolled his eyes.

"And this wedding shall take place this evening?" Baako asked incredulously.

"Oh, I do not know when. I have yet to ask the dear widow," Hossam replied, producing a small white paperboard box from the folds of his galabiya. "I have a gift of candied nuts and dried fruit to sweeten my proposal. God's willing, she will accept."

Now it was Baako's turn to laugh heartily.

"I hope that your proposal will be blessed by acceptance. Goodbye, for now, my friend," he said. "Perhaps the next time we meet you shall be an old married man."

"Old I shall be. Ever older by the day. As we all are. Married? Well, who knows?" He said shrugging his shoulders.

Baako Mustafa hurried toward the meat market to buy a bountiful feast for his dinner. His clients from the United States, the author, wife and friend, would be arriving sometime later tonight or early tomorrow and his meals would change composition and locales over the following ten days.

One day earlier shortly after noontime, Marcus Darke, his wife Valencia, and their friend Sebastian Reckling were feeling the thrust of the engines as their Lockheed L-1649A began rolling down the runway at New York's Idlewild Airport. Their first stop would be London for a change of planes, and then they would fly on into Cairo.

Their overnight flight would be in comfortable First Class, as would their second flight to Cairo.

Adeline and Adam Carter's airplane had just taken off from Rome's airport after changing planes from their London flight. They had just barely made the connection, running as fast as their old legs would allow down the corridors, and were both huffing and puffing as they settled back into their seats. First Class, of course.

The adventure was about to begin.

6

Dusk was beginning to darken the streets, alleys, minarets, and domes of Cairo as Baako Mustafa casually walked through the lobby of the Mena House Hotel. He inhaled the pleasant aroma of Kyphi, his favorite incense. The place was bustling with laughing and chattering guests either arriving back from their daily excursions or getting ready to head out into the city for some nighttime dining and fun. He glanced around but found the door to the small tour office closed. He strode up to the check-in desk.

"Masaa' el Kher, Baako!" said the young lady manning the desk, beaming when she saw the handsome man approach. "We haven't seen you here for a while, have we?"

"Good evening to you, too, Nevine," he replied with a smile. "No, my tour groups have been putting their guests in less expensive hotels in the main city for a while now. Their loss."

They both chuckled.

"Actually, my friend, I have a couple clients flying into Cairo as we speak and they shall be checking in here. Maybe later tonight or early tomorrow morning, depending on flight delays or what have you. Please make sure they get this packet of information," he said as he handed her a white envelope. "I shall assume that they'll be here in time for luncheon tomorrow and let them know I shall meet with them in your terrace dining room at noon."

"Wonderful, Baako," she replied with a wide smile. "They will be so lucky to be in your hands."

Baako glanced around once again at the closed door.

"Maybe I arrived too late this evening. Has Yasmin left already for the day?"

Nevine looked toward the closed office door and sighed.

"Ah, well…Yasmin Ahmed has left for good. Just a few weeks ago she moved to her new job at the Winter Palace in Luxor."

"Oh," Baako replied in astonishment. "Excellent old hotel, such as this one. Well, then, hadh sa'eed (*good luck*) to her. That must have been unexpected?"

"Yes and no, but she has been replaced by her *very* capable assistant. Have you not yet met Manal Khalifa?"

"No, I have not, Nevine, but I surely intend to introduce myself tomorrow."

"It will be a pleasure for both of you, I have no doubt. She is most delightful and far more knowledgeable about our wonderful country than Yasmin."

"Very good, then. I shall look forward to meeting her."

As Baako Mustafa turned to leave he passed among the guests returning from their daily excursions. They looked excited…they looked tired…and they looked overwhelmed. He smiled at them as he walked. An attractive young woman dressed in a long, silky blue galabiya with an emerald hijab on her head was handing them small glasses of refreshing chilled karkade from a large silver tray. Karkade, pronounced car-ka-day, is a deep red tart-sweet herbal tea made from dried hibiscus flower petals.

The woman held out the tray to Baako as he approached and gave him a wide smile and a slight bow. He smiled in return and took one of the glasses.

"It's nice to see you again, Baako. You have been a stranger lately."

"Oh, you'll see a lot more of me in the coming weeks, Zahra," he laughed, downing the glass of karkade in one gulp.

Fifteen minutes later, Marcus Darke, Valencia, and Sebastian Reckling, all looking tired from their long journey, walked through the hotel lobby, luggage in tow, and approached the check-in counter.

"Good evening, sir," Nevine said. And then all of a sudden she recognized the name when he gave it. "Oh, my goodness! You just missed your guide, Baako. He left not too long ago, hoping, perhaps that you had arrived. He left this for you," as she handed the white envelope to Marcus. "You must be exhausted from your journey. Let's get you checked in."

Both Valencia and Sebastian snickered when they heard the name Baako.

"Baako? Sounds like a circus monkey. With a name like Baako, I can just imagine what he looks like," Valencia whispered into Marcus's ear. "Probably a hundred years old, missing a few teeth, walks with a cane and wears those long flowing whatchamacallits they all wear here."

Navine arched an eyebrow and stifled a snicker.

"Don't be so rude, Val," Marcus replied. "He and I have corresponded only via the mail and telegraph, so I have no idea what he looks like. He never described himself to me. No reason, I suppose. I just know that he has a sterling reputation."

They were in for quite a surprise.

"I hope I can get my shoes back on," whimpered Adeline Carter as their airplane taxied to the gate at Cairo Airport in Heliopolis. "My feet are swollen."

Her brother laughed as he helped her up and out of her seat...shoes on...and they shuffled down the crowded aisle to deplane.

As they walked toward customs, their ears were greeted with the sounds of many languages and their eyes were greeted with the sight of passengers, mostly men, in various Arab attire. Countless dozens of men wearing long white robes (dishdasha), and red and white headscarves (ghuthrain) intermingled with those in casual western wear as they all seemed to be racing to get out into the night.

"I can smell their camels already," Adam joked as they continued down the long corridor.

"Behave yourself, Addy," snickered Adeline. "I just hope we won't have to ride one to get to the hotel!"

They both laughed.

It took almost two hours to get through customs, claim their baggage and hire a taxi for the forty-five minute ride to the hotel. The Mena House.

7

The Terrace Dining Room was an expansive outdoor area overlooking a large swimming pool, which was backed by rows of tall palm trees. Unseen birds were noisily calling to one another from the trees. Just beyond the surrounding garden area one could see the hotel's private golf course. The tops of the Great Pyramids could also be seen peeking through the palm fronds. Hungry lunchtime guests, being served by bustling waiters who were wearing flowing galabiyas and turbans on their heads, filled most of the tables. Most of the diners were enjoying the pleasant weather as they chattered like magpies.

Shortly after noon, Marcus, Valencia, and Sebastian had been sitting at their table on the terrace for several minutes when they all turned to see a waiter point someone in their direction. Valencia's eyes widened as the man started walking toward them. He was very tan. He was very handsome. He was wearing loose fitting beige linen trousers, with an equally loose fitting beige long-sleeved open collared shirt, untucked, and dark brown leather sandals.

Several of the other female diners followed the man's stride as well.

"Just a suggestion, Val," Marcus whispered, "you might want to put your eyes back in your head."

"Shut up, smart ass," she whispered back, with a snicker.

The man smiled as he approached their table. Marcus stood up.

"Marhaba…welcome to Cairo," the man said in perfect English with an intriguing Arabic accent. "I am Baako Mustafa."

He reached out to shake Marcus's hand.

"I assume, sir, that you are Marcus Darke."

Sebastian Reckling stood as well.

"I am," answered Marcus, shaking Baako's hand, "and this is my wife Valencia and our good friend Sebastian Reckling.

The two men shook hands and Baako bowed to Valencia who was still sitting...and still staring.

"Please, sit, Baako," said Marcus with a smile, as he gestured to a chair.

"Baako," said Valencia, "what an intriguing name."

"Ah, yes...thank you. Well, Baako means first born. But my parents must have thought that I was perfect right from the start so I am an only child. And, as far as my last name...Mustafa means a chosen person. Apropos, is it not? *You*, Mr. Darke, have chosen *me* to be your guide."

Suddenly, Valencia was feeling *very* guilty about making fun of Baako's name the night before. She fidgeted nervously in her chair, her hands toying with her linen napkin.

Baako Mustafa chuckled as he looked at Valencia.

"I have a feeling, Mrs. Darke, that I am not quite what you were expecting, am I?"

Nevine, the check-in clerk at the front desk the night before, had overheard Valencia's comment about his name, found it quite funny, and told him about it.

Valencia blushed and was a bit flustered. *Was it that obvious?* Valencia thought to herself.

"Well...I...er...perhaps..." she stammered.

Baako laughed, shaking his head.

"No worries, you'll see plenty of those old men in galabiyas and turbans while you're here. I haven't worn one since I was a child, although I might revert back to one years from now in my dotterage."

And with that statement an instant bond was formed between the four people at that table.

"If you intend to place your next murder mystery in my country, Marcus, you may as well keep it factual. I know you like to include many details. I have read your previous books."

"Did you like them?" Marcus Darke asked.

There was a slight pause.

"I read very little fiction, to be honest with you," Baako answered. "Hardly ever, for that matter. Books of your nature have never been on my reading list. Although, simply because of the setting, I thoroughly enjoyed

Death On The Nile. Agatha Christie is a popular author here in Egypt, believe it or not. Our readers here favored that book in particular simply because it was not political in any way."

Again, there was a slight pause.

"To answer your question, yes, I enjoyed your books. Very well written. I hope you won't be offended, Marcus, but I was able to figure out who the killers were in all your books before you actually revealed the culprits. But still, they were quite clever."

Valencia and Sebastian snickered. Marcus looked crestfallen.

"Back to that envelope," Baako said, again pointing to the thick envelope, "There are details in there regarding practically every tomb and temple from Alexandria in the north to Abu Simbel in the south. Far more information than you'll probably need but it should keep you from scurrying to the library when you are writing your book. And, should we visit them while you are here, you won't have to take copious notes as I tell you about the sites. I promise, I won't bore you with tiny details. But I could."

They all laughed at that.

"A couple little things that I didn't put in that envelope. I just thought of one as I now see you. As you can imagine, blonde women are a rarity here in Egypt. So, Valencia, please don't be too alarmed if you get many, many stares as we walk through the streets and sites. Also, friendship is very deep among men here. Don't be shocked to see two men walking hand-in-hand out in public. Even the military or the police. It's not what you might think. It's just that they are very good friends."

"Don't you *even* think about it, Reckless," Marcus joked. "I like you, but not *that* much!"

The laughter was raucous with that statement. Sebastian shot Marcus a one-finger salute.

"I have a question," Sebastian began. "I know that this is a Muslim country, but I noticed that there is a lounge with a bar here in the hotel. And it was crowded last night when we checked in. I'm a bit confused and conflicted. Not that I'm a lush, or anything, but is alcohol permitted here in Egypt?"

Baako couldn't help but laugh.

"*Theoretically* speaking, alcohol is not present here in Egypt," he answered. "In practice, it *is*. We Egyptians have been brewing beer, for example, for over three thousand years. There are strict regulations, however. The sale and consumption of alcohol is strictly forbidden in public places...with the exception, that is, of hotels and tourist facilities. Religion aside, our authorities aren't stupid. Tourists love to drink...and spend money. Personally I do not consume alcohol, but I have been told that the bar here makes the best Gin Rickey in town. So, later you all may enjoy an evening cocktail or two...or a glass of wine out here on the terrace if you so desire. No fear of reprisals or deportation."

"Well, that's a relief," sighed Valencia. "Not that *I'm* a lush or anything!"

"Outstanding! Tonight, then, I shall pretend to be the late, Great Jay Gatsby with a Gin Rickey, old sport!" Marcus declared.

The three Americans all laughed. Baako had no idea who the Great Jay Gatsby is...or was.

"Egypt is an adventure," Baako Mustafa continued. "Today is a day of rest for you after your long journey here. Take advantage of the relaxation. Tomorrow is another matter. There is much to see and do. I know I sent you a proposed itinerary but where would *you* like to start?"

"The pyramids, of course, are so enticing," answered Marcus without hesitation. "We saw them from our bedroom windows. And there they are" he said pointing to the tops of the structures beyond the palm trees. "Magnificent. Breathtaking. Can we climb them?"

Baako sat back and pondered the question with a slight frown.

"It is definitely not advisable, but some do. It's very rigorous and best done by the young."

Sebastian sat upright in a hurry. He and Marcus exchanged glances.

"What the hell! Are you inferring that *we're* too old?" Marcus asked incredulously. "Have *you* climbed them?"

"Yes, I have climbed the pyramid of Khufu. Several times. It takes strong legs and strong arms. And definitely *not* having a fear of heights. I should warn you, it would be like climbing a building forty-six stories in height...but on the outside. Even though it is January, it's best done early, just after dawn, to avoid the later heat of the day."

"Good!" Marcus exclaimed loudly, clapping his hands together. "Then I challenge Reckless to a race to the top! Tomorrow at dawn, it is!"

8

Just before leaving the Mena House, Baako checked to see if the new manager of the tour office was at her desk. She was.

He peeked in the door and she was sitting at her desk having an animated conversation with an elderly couple. There was a lot of pleasant laughter, which made Baako smile. The couple was handed a small envelope and they stood up to leave. He could hear the couple, both thanking the manager, and both with a British accent. The couple nodded and smiled at Baako as they passed and walked down the hall.

Baako Mustafa smiled as he entered the small office. He bowed slightly as the beautiful young woman stood up. She smiled and bowed slightly as well.

"Masaa' el-kheer, I am Baako Mustafa," he said boldly.

She reached out her hand to him and gave a little giggle.

"Good afternoon to you, too, Baako Mustafa. Your reputation precedes you," she said with a lilting accent.

She was wearing a white linen blouse over beige linen trousers. Her long black hair was tied back into a long single braid that flowed down her back. Her earrings looked as though they had been made from Egyptian coins. Baako noticed that she was wearing a popular amulet hanging from a thin chain around her neck. It was the Eye of Horus.

The Eye of Horus represents protection, health, and restoration. It figures greatly in the Egyptian legend of Isis and Osiris. The amulet was also worn to ward off evil actions by the Djinn.

Baako Mustafa laughed.

"I hope that it's a *good* reputation that precedes me. Otherwise I shall deny everything."

The young lady laughed and shook her head.

"No need for denial, Baako…and my name is Manal Khalifa, by the way."

They held each other's eyes for a brief moment.

It may have been *brief*, but it was long enough for Baako Mustafa to become smitten.

He may not have realized it just then, but so had Manal.

Neither one had ever felt like this before.

Baako bowed slightly once again.

"I'm glad we had the chance to meet, Manal. I haven't been to the Mena House for a while. I'll be here practically at dawn in the morning, however."

Manal gave him a quizzical look.

"Yes, I have been hired as the guide for three of your current guests and two of them insist on racing each other to the top of the Pyramid of Khufu."

Manal gasped.

"Surely you warned them of the potential dangers, right?"

"To a certain degree. I suspect, however, that there is more to this rivalry than a race to the top of a pyramid."

The elderly couple that had just left the office had been Adeline Carter and her brother Adam.

"Did you notice that necklace that the lady was wearing?" Adam asked.

"Oh, I *did*, dear…I certainly did. Unusual. Stunning," Adeline responded enthusiastically. "I most definitely need *that* one in my collection."

Adam chuckled.

"I'll see what I can do, my dear. Be patient."

Manal Khalifa had given the couple some vouchers for an evening of entertainment in Cairo. A hantoor (horse carriage ride) from the hotel through the historic sections of Cairo. An exciting journey after dark. And then a couple of hours sailing the Nile up and down around Cairo on one of the small sailboats called feluccas. Another exciting excursion as the lights of Cairo danced across the skittering waters. The Carter twins were excited. They would be in contact with several other tourists this evening... close contact...and Adeline and Adam were sure they would be returning to the hotel with a nice stash from their unsuspecting fellow travelers. Who would *ever* be suspicious of an elderly, doddering British couple?

It was shortly after 1 A.M. when their old carriage driver awoke them to tell them they were back at the hotel. He chuckled loudly as the two people, even older than him, appeared befuddled as they slowly awoke and stepped down from the carriage. His horse whinnied as the carriage wobbled in their departure. Adam Carter shook the driver's hand, presented him with a sizable tip and thanked him for the exceptional evening. The driver, Hossam Mahfouz, had been so knowledgeable, expounding facts as he slowly drove them through Casaba, the oldest part of the city, down Muizz Street, one of the oldest in Cairo, and allowing them time to tour through Khan el-Khalili market. He was very definitive in his warning about the two of them walking through the bazaar.

"Be wary," he had cautioned as they started to head into the area, "This place is filled with wonderful prizes...as well as devious pickpockets... many of them my friends." And he laughed.

Adeline and Adam Carter had smiled and thanked him for the warning. They then had winked at each other as they headed into the crowded marketplace.

Once the twins were safely behind the door of their suite, they smiled and did a little jig in celebration. It had been a very rewarding evening... aside from seeing the sights and being told some Egyptian history by a grizzled old carriage driver.

Adeline had carried a large purse throughout the evening, clutching it to her ample breasts as she walked. Adam wore a double-breasted jacket that had many pockets, none of which had been picked during their excursion but many of them had been filled as the evening progressed.

They both sat on the edge of Adam's bed and emptied their treasures out on the bedspread. Adeline gasped as Adam produced four Rolex watches, an inexpensive Bulova with a scratched crystal, a wad of cash in various denominations from a half-dozen different countries, a gold necklace, and one diamond brooch.

"I can't imagine," exclaimed Adam, "why any sensible tourist would travel to a country like this wearing such expensive jewelry. They were just asking for it, as far as I'm concerned. Serves them right, it does."

And they both chuckled.

Adeline's oversized purse contained several silver, gold, and brass trinkets she had shoplifted from a few of the markets in Khan el-Khalili. No one ever suspects little old ladies of doing such devious things, even the wily shopkeepers in a marketplace well known for such devious things.

"Goodness," Adeline said with a sigh as her eyes scanned the pile of goodies before her. "I'm certainly glad we declined the trip on that little sailboat thing. Just the two of us and a skipper? How boring and unrewarding it would have been."

"Oh, but I would have liked it, Addy," answered Adam. "Some other time perhaps. Before we leave for home."

9

Dawn. The sun had yet to break the horizon and Fajr, the first calls to morning prayers by a muezzin, could be heard from a distant minaret. The chilly early morning air met the warmth of the desert sands and little puffs of misty fog drifted around the pyramids.

Baako Mustafa was waiting patiently in the hotel lobby for the two gentlemen to appear from their rooms. Although he was never in the military, Baako was wearing light beige fatigues, a tight brown T-shirt that showed off his muscular arms and toned chest, and ankle-high sandy-brown desert boots. Covering his head and shoulders was a traditional keffiyeh, protecting him from the sun and possible wind. He was ready for the hefty climb.

The hotel was beginning to wake up. Guests were milling about, some heading to the breakfast dining room. He smelled the aroma of coffee coming from somewhere, mixed with sandalwood incense. Soon he could hear the voices of the two men as they exited the long hallway leading from some guestrooms and walked briskly toward him.

They stopped in their tracks as Baako stood up to greet them.

"Wow," said Marcus Darke, eyeing their guide up and down. "You look so...rugged and outdoorsy!"

Baako laughed.

The two men were wearing dungarees rolled up at the cuff and loose-fitting white T-shirts. They each had black and white Keds on their feet and NY Yankees baseball caps on their heads.

"And you both look so...American!"

A few moments later a perky Valencia practically bounced down the hall to join them, carrying a Rolleiflex single-lens reflex camera within a camera case slung over her shoulder. She was a bit better dressed for the hot desert sun. But *just* a bit. She was wearing loose-fitting white cotton slacks, a canary yellow long-sleeved blouse with a wide-brimmed floppy yellow hat to match...and white Keds.

"Wow," she said as she saw Baako. "You look so..."

"Don't say it, Val," said Marcus under his breath. "Just. Don't."

"I *told* you, Marcus, that you and Reckless should have gone to Abercrombie and Fitch!"

They both chuckled.

Fifteen minutes later, after a short walk from the hotel, they were all standing at the base of the Great Pyramid of Khufu.

"Jesus Christ!" Sebastian Reckling said, staring straight up at the massive structure. "Looks a bit different up close, doesn't it?"

"Changing your mind, Reckless?" snickered Marcus Darke.

"No, no...not at all," Reckling responded, although with a slight bit of hesitation.

"Alright, guys," Valencia chimed in, "I want a picture of the three of you together before the climb."

She posed them, side by side, at the base of the pyramid, showing that the massive blocks were almost as tall as each of the men, and then snapping a few photos. Marcus put his arm up on the side of one of the limestone blocks, looking both right and then left.

"How many of these things are there?" he asked in amazement.

"It has been estimated that there are over two million of these limestone and granite blocks here. Could be more," Baako responded.

"How the *hell* did they do it?" Sebastian asked.

Baako Mustafa laughed.

"Ah, that is a secret...a *big* secret. If I told you I'd have to kill you."

"You don't know *either*, do you?" Marcus chuckled, cocking his head.

Baako smiled.

"At the moment, that is true, sir. You are correct. I do *not* know. Not for sure anyway. I have my theories, but so do many others. In time we will discover the secret. These structures certainly demonstrated the Egyptians' skills in astronomy, mathematics, logistics and engineering. But now *we* are wasting time. The sun is swiftly rising. It will be very hot by the time we reach the top. Gentlemen, shall we?"

"Show us how, Baako, and we'll follow!" Marcus hollered.

"Please, *please* be careful, Marcus!" Valencia called out with a bit of trepidation as she stared up toward the top. She never thought they would go through with it once they were this close to the towering pyramids. "I love you, darling!"

"I love you, too, sweetie pie!" Marcus called back.

Sebastian Reckling rolled his eyes.

Baako Mustafa placed both hands on one of the blocks, swung his right leg up until his knee rested on the stone and easily hoisted himself up onto the first block...and then pulling himself up onto the next...and then the next. Already three levels up.

"Shit," Marcus exclaimed. "Valencia said his name sounded like a circus monkey and look at that showoff go! Scampering up those damn things like a...circus monkey! Come on, Reckless, let's go."

Valencia snapped a couple more photographs as the men started their ascent. Now she was almost afraid to watch.

A little puff of misty fog drifted by, momentarily shielding Valencia from seeing the three men as they scampered up the pyramid. At this point, neither Marcus nor Sebastian found the climb taxing, but they both realized that if they took one wrong step they would be history.

They turned to look down for a brief moment but the fog obscured the ground. It was at that very point that Sebastian Reckling learned, for the first time, that he had a fear of heights. Not being able to see the ground, even for a slight moment, terrified him.

And then the fog drifted away and he could see the ground once again. They were not even near halfway up and the height seemed dizzying. Valencia, with her camera pointing right at him, seemed so distant. So small.

"Come on, Reckless, don't stop now!" Marcus Darke called from a few levels up. "I think that the circus monkey has made it to the top already!"

Baako Mostafa had *not* made it to the top just yet. The careful climb would take about two hours.

Reckling started climbing once again but, in the back of his mind, he wondered how he would ever get back down again.

The sun was climbing higher and Baako had been right. It was getting hotter. Both men were beginning to sweat. They didn't know if it was really from the heat or the exertion.

Sebastian had to stop and rest for a moment once again. Although he didn't really want to, he looked down toward the sands below. A man wearing a flowing galabiya and a red turban was leading a camel with a rope. He approached Valencia. Sebastian could see her shake her head, but then raised the camera to take a photograph. The old Egyptian held out his hand toward her. She reached into her pocket and gave him something. The man, obliging with the picture taking, had said "Bakshish, bakshish", meaning "tip, tip"...and she understood by handing him a few coins. The man was apparently satisfied and meandered on his way, looking for another tourist who might want to ride his camel.

Sebastian was suddenly thrown off-balance as a flock of pigeons flew past him...*below* him, which disoriented him. Birds flying *below* him... not a usual vantage point. He gripped the huge block of limestone as he began to feel dizzy. He quickly sat down.

He heard a strange noise to his left and a large brownish-grey bird, with a solid reddish spot on the back of its head stared at him. It had a hooked grey beak and thin yellow circles around its black eyes. It was sitting on the block next to where Sebastian was sitting. The bird looked up at him and hopped a bit closer.

"What the hell do *you* want?" Sebastian asked the bird.

"What the *hell* are you doing, Reckless?" Marcus Darke yelled from several levels above him. "You can rest your sorry ass once you get up to the top. It's looking great up here."

Sebastian looked at the bird that then ruffled its feathers and flew away with a loud screech.

Sebastian Reckling sighed, turned toward the stones and once again began to climb. The early morning fog had totally dissipated and the temperature was continuing to climb. Even though it was January and the early mornings could get quite chilly, the afternoon sun always generated pleasant heat in the low to mid 70s.

"Wow!" Marcus exclaimed as he looked down to the ground from the opposite side of the pyramid that Sebastian was climbing. "That's the Sphinx down there, isn't it? Sure looks small from up here."

Baako laughed and shook his head.

"*Everything* looks small from up here," he replied.

Twenty minutes later, Sebastian Reckling joined Marcus and Baako on the top of the impressive structure. The square flat top "platform" consisted of small blocks of broken limestone; ten roughly cut, uneven bricks across in one direction and ten rows of uneven bricks in the other. It was a *very* small area. From this vantage point, they could look down at all four sides of the pyramid. A stiff wind was blowing that felt refreshing after their climb.

"Took you long enough, Reckless," Marcus laughed. "But I have to admit, we're both using muscles we probably never used before. We'll be sore tonight."

"I warned you," Baako snickered.

"Some crazy-ass bird came along and sat down beside me," Sebastian said. "It was probably trying to coax me to fly...or jump."

Baako laughed.

"Ah, yes. I saw it down there next to you. That was a Lanner Falcon. They live here in the Western Desert. I have no doubt he was a distant relative of our very own falcon-headed god...Horus. One of our many gods."

"Oh, yeah?" Asked Marcus. "What does *that* god...Horus, do?"

"Many things, Marcus. But one of them is that Horus is a protector of one's health and wellbeing. So you see, Sebastian, should Marcus, here, had wanted to push you off the pyramid, Horus would have protected you."

Marcus Darke blushed. He remembered what he had said to Valencia back in New York. But it had only been in jest.

"Perhaps, Marcus," Baako continued, "you might be able to include that in your next murder mystery."

"Don't be getting any ideas, Marc-ass," Sebastian laughed. "Baako is a witness."

Sebastian cautiously inched his way back over to the very edge of the top platform, looking down to the sands of the Western Desert far below. He waved to Valencia and she waved back, aiming her camera upwards. A sudden gust of wind blew off his baseball cap and he made a grab for it.

That's when he tripped over a small, uneven block of limestone and fell.

10

Marcus Darke reacted instantly, swiftly reaching out and grabbing Sebastian Reckling by the back of his T-shirt. Baako Mustafa was equally as swift, grabbing Marcus around his waist with two arms and pulling both men back onto the top surface while fighting to maintain his *own* balance. Marcus's heart was beating so hard at this point he could almost hear it. Sebastian, breathing heavily, felt as though he was either going to faint or vomit. He did neither. He just plopped himself down onto the hard stone.

Lachmah, Baako thought to himself. *Awkward. Clumsy.*

"Going back down will be much easier and faster than the climb up," Baako said, "but I wouldn't recommend what you did just there."

Sebastian Reckling stared at Baako for a moment. "That's it," he said, "Either send up a helicopter to get me off this thing or I'm simply staying up here until I die. Bring me food and water. Is that too much to ask?"

Getting down from the top was, indeed, much easier than getting up. The men waited until Sebastian regained his composure and then, fifteen minutes later, they began their descent. It was simply a matter of sitting down on a block of the limestone and sliding off to the next level below. Looking practically straight down from that very top was dizzying, though, and the men still had to maintain their balance as they landed on the surface of the blocks so as not to fall forward.

Baako made it look easy. It *was* easy...well, easier...but Marcus and Sebastian still took their time in sliding from one level to the next.

Two hours later they felt the desert sands beneath their feet once again. Sebastian felt like crying. But he didn't. Their T-shirts clung to their chests

Marc D. Hasbrouck

wet with sweat while the backsides of their dungarees were worn thin. And they were both sunburnt.

Valencia, who had been roaming around the vast area for the last few hours taking photographs, came running up to greet the trio.

"Well, did you guys have fun? It must have been awesome up there!"

"Oh, the term awesome doesn't even come close," answered Marcus. *Reckless definitely earned his nickname up there*, he thought to himself.

Baako Mustafa could only shake his head and laugh. He started to walk back toward their hotel.

"Oh, wait," called Valencia, "I need another picture of you guys after your little adventure."

"I need to pee," Sebastian said with an exasperated sigh. "Make it fast!"

"And I need a drink!" exclaimed Marcus Darke.

Almost at that exact same moment, Adeline and Adam Carter had stopped in at the Tourist Relations office in the Mena House to see Manal Khalifa. Adeline handed the young woman a little white envelope.

"Here, dear," she said, "we're returning the vouchers for the ride on that little sailboat on the Nile. Adam and I were too tired to take it last night. Your talkative carriage driver kept us out quite late."

"Oh," explained Manal, "those vouchers are open-ended. If you like, you can still use them. But I have a better idea."

The Carter twins just looked at her.

"I'm taking my two little nephews on one of these feluccas this evening. They've never been on one. Why don't you accompany us? I can even tell you a little bit about what we'll be seeing as we sail through Cairo."

Manal was again wearing that beautiful necklace with the amulet that Adeline had admired.

The twins looked at one another and smiled.

"Why, that would be lovely, dear," Adeline purred. "You're so sweet. What a delightful and thoughtful invitation."

"Wonderful," Manal replied. "Leave with me this evening, then, at six. "It will be fun!"

As the Carter twins headed back out into the hotel lobby three men and a woman passed them. Two of the men were sweaty and, one in

48

particular, looked disgruntled. One of the men was obviously Egyptian. The other two men and the woman were very obviously American.

Swaffham, England

At that exact moment, it was mid morning on what *had* been a quiet little street. Wendling Road. The mailbox of Eudora Smythe was filled to overflowing and the postman had grown quite suspicious. He knew that she was fastidious to the point of the extreme and always collected her mail almost as soon as it was delivered. He felt guilty for not acting upon this sooner. Earlier in the day he had approached the front door with trepidation. He rang the doorbell. Repeatedly. He then knocked on the door. Loudly. There was a faint, but distinctly foul aroma seemingly coming from behind the door. There were sidelights on either side of the door and he cautiously peeked in. He could see in through the tiny house to a part of a kitchen. Something…or someone was lying on the floor. He let out a gasp.

There was a classic red Gilbert Scott telephone box at the far corner of the street and he ran to it.

Twenty minutes later, the constables arrived and forced open the front door. The postman stood back and waited. The stench, unmistakable and sickening, coming from inside the house made him retch.

Within minutes a strip of blue and white plastic tape — POLICE LINE DO NOT CROSS — hung across the front door.

The medical examiner would later determine that Eudora Smythe had been dead for perhaps a little over two weeks. Under her odoriferous decomposing right hand was found a slip of paper where she had obviously begun to write something when she died. There was only one word: ADELINE.

Marcus Darke and Sebastian Reckling went straight back to their respective rooms, quickly showered and changed clothes. Marcus, followed shortly by Reckless, joined Valencia and Baako out in the terrace dining room. Baako had removed his keffiyeh and looked none the worse for wear from the strenuous climb. Valencia and Baako were each sipping glasses of chilled karkade and two glasses of the refreshing drink sat at the places reserved for the two other gentlemen.

Reckless swallowed the karkade practically in one gulp. And sat back into his chair focusing on nothing in particular.

"Reckless," said Valencia with a little smile on her face, "Baako was telling me about your..."

"I don't wish to discuss it!" Reckless said abruptly in a tone a bit too terse for even him.

Marcus winked at his wife and Baako stifled a snicker.

Following a long, somewhat awkward pause, Baako cleared his throat.

"Alright, Marcus," he started, "now that we have *that* little adventure behind us, let's discuss what you hope to accomplish within the next week or so. I am well aware that you...along with Valencia...do an extraordinary amount of research for your novels. I'm curious. Your previous books include various murders, their perpetrators, and their motives. I don't read such books as yours. Tell me more about murder. I assume you both have researched *that* topic extensively."

"We have, indeed," replied Marcus Darke with a nod. "And we include our...ahem...*clumsy* friend here quite often. Reckless, here, is an authority of all sorts on criminals, so to speak. But, regarding murder itself?"

Marcus collected his thoughts and sipped his karkade.

"Yes, we *have* done extensive research on the matter. Here are some things we discovered. Most murders are solved within the first forty-eight hours. That's true. Why? Because most murderers don't know what the hell they are doing. They're sloppy. They're careless. They lash out in anger, perhaps...or jealousy. A burglary or robbery gone badly. It's a spontaneous action...or reaction, if you will. By the time they think about fingerprints, alibis, or blood splatter, it's too late. They have already left the clues. They're idiots. There have been serial killers scattered about throughout history. Serial killers, by the way, are ninety-one percent male perpetrators."

He swirled what was left of his karkade in his glass. The bright red liquid almost looked like blood.

"Ah..." he began once again. "And *then* you have what happens once in a very rare while. Hardly ever, for that matter. The *perfect* murder. A seemingly unsolvable crime. Ah, yes. A perfect murder takes time. Time to plot out one's steps and not be careless, or clumsy…or, haha," he chuckled, "reckless. Premeditated murder. Calculated. Patient.

"Being a trained forensic linguist," Sebastian Reckling interjected, "I listen to what the accused…or sometimes *not* accused…individuals say. How they say it. What they *don't* say…how they sit or stand or twitch."

"Interesting," Baako Mustafa said with a tilt to his head. "But, tell me now, what kind of murder mystery do you intend to take place in our glorious land here?"

Marcus sat back and thought for a moment.

"Well," he began, "Agatha Christie did a wonderful job with *Death on the Nile*, but I might try something involving your current politics. I've been studying recently about the Egyptian people getting tired of British occupation."

"Indeed," Baako said, but with trepidation. "You may be here at a potentially dangerous time."

"On the other hand," Marcus continued, "Prior to coming here, Valencia discovered, in her research, about a couple of intriguing Egyptian serial killers. What were their names, Val? Can you remember?"

"Yes, vividly," Valencia Darke answered. "Two siblings. Sisters. Raya and Sakina. Along with their husbands they killed seventeen women. That was back in 1919."

"Jesus Christ," Marcus exclaimed. "Can you seriously believe that? How rare could *that* be? Siblings as serial killers. Weird, huh? I can't even imagine what kind of family *they* must have been raised in."

"I sure would have loved to have been around to interview *those* two!" Sebastian Reckling exclaimed. "What a case study that would be."

Baako Mustafa was dumbfounded.

"Somehow, in my Egyptian history classes I missed that! But…do you intend to write a contemporary story as you just hinted, or perhaps set your murder back in time. To the time of our pharaohs?"

Marcus Darke furrowed his brow.

"Huh…" he said with a quizzical look on his face. "You know, I never thought of *that*."

"Perhaps you might know already that Cleopatra came from a long line of killers," Baako said, "and she continued the family tradition. She murdered her siblings, among several others. I mentioned Agatha Christie earlier. Were you aware that she and her archeologist husband spent a lot of time here in Egypt? Our country fascinated her and she did, indeed, write a lesser-known mystery set here in 2000 B.C., *Death Comes As The End*. It contains a high number of murders. I suggest you may want to check that one out before you write *yours*, Marcus."

Marcus just stared at Baako in amazement.

"Baako, you're a walking encyclopedia," he exclaimed. "No wonder you're such a popular guide. You scare the shit outta me!"

Baako Mustafa smiled. And then he chuckled.

"We are just beginning our journey together, Marcus. I have many… *many* more stories to impart. Perhaps you will think much differently of me by the time all of you leave Egypt."

The group sat silent for a few moments as Marcus stared off into the near-distance.

"You need some local color, as the term goes, Marcus," Baako said, breaking the silence. "This afternoon we'll take a short trip to where you can rub elbows with our teeming masses. I shall take you to Khan el-Khalili, a souk…a bazaar. If you're lucky, we might be able to find a good old friend of mine. By old, I mean *old*. He has stories that you won't believe. *Don't* believe them. Most of them are fabrications. But he will delight you anyway. Maybe he knows about your sibling killers."

11

Baako Mostafa led the trio of Americans through the labyrinthian alleyways of Khan el-Khalili. Various vendors called out to Baako as they walked and he responded in kind, waving at each one.

"You're certainly a popular guy, aren't you?" Valencia said, glancing around at all the markets as they walked.

"A well known one, anyway," Baako answered.

They all strolled further into the souk.

"Ahh, and there he sits", said Baako when he spotted his friend at his favorite curbside table at the coffee house. And his old friend, Hossam Mahfouz, spotted him as well.

"Baako! Salam 'alaykum…hello, my friend!" the old man called out, waving his hand wildly.

"Wa 'alaykum is salam," responded Baako.

Baako introduced the three Americans to his friend who greeted them warmly.

"My friend," Baako said, "are you now an old married man?"

Hossam Mahfouz shrugged his shoulder and threw up both hands.

"Old, yes, my friend," he answered, "married, no. She refused. The widow say she would never take a carriage driver for a husband. She say I smell like horse."

Baako laughed and winked at his companions.

"There are worse smells. But, Hossam, you seem to spend more time *here* than with your horse and carriage."

The old man once again shrugged his shoulder and threw up his hands.

"I brought my companions, Hossam, to hear some of your stories. Your fables of times past. Marcus Darke is the author I told you about and he's doing research for his next novel."

Hossam Mahfouz drew back, taking a long look at Marcus.

"So...*you* are the one who may rattle the Djinn and cause trouble, are you?"

Marcus looked at Baako.

"I have *no* idea what he just said."

Again, Baako laughed.

"Listen and he will explain. Remember what I told you. Believe what you will. I believe very little."

Hossam Mahfouz folded his arms across his chest.

"My friends here, Hossam, are staying at the Mena House before we head off into Upper Egypt."

"Ah, yes...mumtaz...excellent old hotel. I was there just last night. I drove a couple of guests, an old couple, around town for several hours. Manal Khalifa hired me to escort them. Have you met Manal, Baako? She is somewhat new at the hotel, I think."

"I met her briefly," Baako answered. "Beautiful woman."

"Ah, yes...then you *have* met her," laughed the old man. "A goddess she is. I shall be back there again tonight. She is taking that old couple into town again. This time for a short sail on the Nile."

"Really? Hmm..." Baako said with a smile on his face and a little twinkle in his eye.

Marcus, Valencia, and Sebastian were getting a little restless. Baako could sense it.

"Hossam, my friend, give Marcus some reasons to include you as a character in his book. Tell him some of the tales you have told me over the years."

Hossam Mahfouz gladly spent the next hour talking. And Talking... and talking. Marcus was enthralled. Valencia was delighted. And Sebastian counted all the potential lies. Marcus was especially intrigued by the Djinn and wondered how he might weave a bit of mysticism into his next book.

Hossam wound up his story telling by recounting his trip through Cairo the night before with the "old couple" from the Mena House. There was something a bit odd about them but he couldn't put his finger on it.

"But I will see them again this evening," he said. "Perhaps you will meet them at your hotel sometime."

Baako was interested in getting back to the Mena House and speaking with Manal as quickly as possible.

Although, of course, neither one had any way of knowing it at this time, but a murderer and an author were soon to meet.

Swaffham, England

It was shortly after noontime and Detective Chief Inspector Weldon Atherstone was back in the home of the deceased Eudora Smythe. Something did not sit right with him about her death. Although the initial investigation found no obvious signs of foul play, he was certain that her death was *not* by natural causes. What did that one-word note, ADELINE, signify?

Her body had long since been removed but the lingering putrid aroma of the dead prevailed. That was a bit odd. It should have dissipated. He had not ventured up the stairs in the small house until now. He thought that there hadn't been a reason to do so. As he climbed the stairs, the strong aroma seemed to grow even stronger.

The room at the top of the stairs, on the left, was a small bathroom. Ugly pink tiles on the walls and floors, with a big, pink bathtub behind pink shower curtains. At least the towels hanging on the racks were white, as was the small, round fluffy rug on the floor. The faucet over the basin had a slow drip. He noticed little things like that. He walked a bit further down the hall, past a small room that appeared to be a sewing room. Sewing machine and several bolts of fabric with a variety of patterns and motifs. There were several poster boards leaning up against the wall with swatches of fabric pinned to them. Was the deceased a decorator?

The next room was a small bedroom. The bed appeared neatly made. Artwork hanging on the walls looked like the kind of cheap, generic themes of nature sold at Woolworth's. Draperies were open, letting in the bright sunlight. And this is where the aroma was the most pungent.

Nothing out of the ordinary that he could see offhand as he turned, looking around the room. He cautiously opened the closet door. Nothing but clothing hanging neatly on their hangers, shoes lined up below, a few hats on a rack above. Everything unpretentious, nothing expensive.

He decided to bend down and look under the bed.

"What the bloody hell is *that*?" Weldon said out loud to no one but himself, as he jumped back.

He stood up quickly and pulled the single bed aside so he could see what the misshapen lump of fur could be.

It was a cat. Or what was left of it. A decomposed mess of fur and bones that was once a Persian grey. Probably dead as long as its mistress. And possibly died the same way, as he would soon discover. There was another lump of something near the cat. It looked like a piece of very moldy, crusty bread.

Cairo, Egypt: 6 P.M.

Adeline and Adam Carter walked down the short hallway in the hotel toward Manal Khalifa's office. She was just locking her door, but she was not alone. The tall Egyptian man and the three Americans were with her.

"What do you suppose *that* means, Addy?" Adeline asked with a worried look on her face. "Are we not going to be alone with her and those children this evening?"

Adam shrugged his shoulders as they proceeded to approach the small group.

"Oh, good! There you are," Manal said with a huge smile on her face. "This is going to turn out to be a wonderful evening for you. Unfortunately, *my* plans have abruptly changed."

She introduced the American trio to the British couple, with the usual pleasantries all around.

"Your horse and carriage should be outside by now," Manal said with a glow of excitement. "I have an urgent family matter that needs attention. You shall go for a leisurely sail up and down the Nile for a short while and then Baako has graciously promised to treat you all to a very special dinner later at one of his favorite restaurants. I wish I could join you, but Baako will be a real treasure trove of information. Please accept my apologies for the change in plans. Well, for *me*, anyway.""

"Oh…" said Adeline with little emotion. "Oh! How very…special. It should be…delightful. And will the little children not be with us either?"

"No, I'm sorry. My nephews will be unavailable this evening as well."

Sebastian Reckling, having difficulty ever pushing his profession aside, was paying very close attention to the way Adeline was speaking and watching her body language. He could sense that her words were not matching her true feelings.

"Well, then," said Adam, "Addy and I will be *delighted*. What an unexpected evening this will turn out to be."

It could be a bonanza, Adam thought to himself, *or a bust*.

Sebastian had the same reaction when Adam Carter spoke. *Perhaps it's just that old folks don't like an unexpected change in plans*, he thought. *I've seen that often.*

12

Baako Mustafa sat next to his friend Hossan Mahfouz up front in the carriage. He smiled at the driver after the others had been seated and nodded his head.

"Let's go, my friend," he said as Hossan then cracked the whip.

Hossan Mahfouz had selected his best looking, most impressive horse and his oldest, classic carriage for this evening. It must have been at least fifty years old, well polished and had a big black leather fold-down canopy. The canopy was folded back down, unnecessary for tonight's ride. It sat the five passengers comfortably in two rows facing each other. The Carters, the heaviest (and widest) of the group sat in the seats directly behind the driver and Baako, facing the three Americans.

The conversation between the passengers began friendly and innocuous, but it eventually took a strange twist.

"Are you enjoying your holiday so far?" Adeline asked the trio, to no one in particular.

"Oh, yes," Valencia answered. "Reckless...I mean, Sebastian had a bit of a jolt on one of the pyramids, but *that* will give us something to laugh about for years to come."

"Reckless? What did you mean? Was he reckless?" Adam Carter asked.

Sebastian chuckled.

"No. Well, yes, I was. But my nickname since college days has been Reckless. I guess I am. As these two will keep reminding me."

"So you are longtime friends, then, I take it," Adeline said to Sebastian, cocking her head. "And the three of you are traveling together. Hmm. Have you no wife?"

There was a pause.

"Not yet, Mrs. Carter," he answered.

"Oh, we're not..." Adam Carter started to say.

Adeline interrupted him quickly.

"Well, there's time then, isn't it, dear?" And she smiled.

"How long have you two been married?" Valencia asked Adeline.

"We're..." Adam began once again, only to be cut off very swiftly by Adeline.

"Seems like forever, dear, doesn't it, Addy?" As she gave her brother a look. They exchanged a secret smile.

"Yes, Addy, it does," he responded, just leaving it there.

"Oh, how cute is that?" gushed Valencia. "You call each other Addy. I get It. Adam and Adeline. That's precious. And I can see that the old cliché is certainly true."

"What cliché is that, dear?" Adeline asked.

"Well, I've heard that the longer couples are married...and I mean decades...they begin to resemble one another. And I can clearly see that in you two. I hope you don't take that the wrong way."

Adam and Adeline both laughed.

"Oh, no...we've been told that for years," Adam replied.

The carriage was being slowed down by automobile traffic as it neared the main part of the city. Car horns were honking and headlights were flashing. Dozens of cars were going in haphazard ways all over the roadway.

"Don't be alarmed by all that racket and confusion," Baako told the group. "No one obeys any traffic laws here. I'm not sure there *are* any traffic laws in Cairo. If someone wants to make a turn, left *or* right, they simply honk their horns repeatedly and flash their lights. And then they go, hoping for the best."

Hossam Mahfouz laughed loudly and turned around to face his passengers.

"This is where I close my eyes and hope my horse is smarter...or faster than anyone else on the road."

"God's willing," said Baako, "we shall be at the dock in about ten minutes."

Marcus Darke reacted as though a thought just popped into his head.

"Carter! Your last name is *Carter.* Sheer coincidence, I'm sure, but any chance you're related to that Carter guy...Howard Carter...who discovered Tutankhamun's tomb back in '22?"

The Carter twins sat silent for the briefest of moments.

"Why, yes…as a matter of fact that's why we traveled here to Egypt," Adam Carter lied. "He was a distant cousin. And our…I mean, *my* father played with Howard when they were tikes. I met him when I was younger and I seem to remember him as a jovial type. Full of jokes and fun when he bounced me on his knee. Yes, fond memories."

Baako Mustafa, who had been intently listening furrowed his brow, but said nothing.

Yes, Howard Carter was a well known archaeologist and Egyptologist who would long be remembered for his amazing find in the Valley of the Kings. But the man was far from jovial and fun loving. He was often abrasive, had a hot temper and had several disputes with Egyptian authorities. He never had any close relationships, was a stoic loner, never married, was possibly homosexual, disliked children immensely, and when he died at the age of sixty-four from Hodgkin's lymphoma a mere nine people attended his funeral.

Baako and Hossam exchanged glances. Baako discretely shook his head as he looked into his friend's eyes and put his index finger to his lips, indicating *say nothing*.

"As fate would have it," Adam continued, embellishing his lie further, "Adeline and I found an old house we really liked a few years back and bought it. It's in the same little town where dear cousin Howard was from. Swaffham, it is. Little old Swaffham. We scrimped and saved over the years for our last hoorah, so to speak, and to come visit the sites where history was made. We both feel as though we are already being treated like royalty…especially with all of you this evening. It makes us old age pensioners giddy, doesn't it, Addy?"

Adeline dabbed at her eyes with a hanky she had in her oversized purse and simply nodded…adding a little sniffle for effect. It was quite an act.

Sebastian Reckling sat back and looked at the two Carters. He had been only half listening at first, but he had been observing. He watched them both as Adam finished with his story. Something intrigued him, though.

"Interesting," he said. "Not only do you two resemble each other, but your speech patterns and gestures are extremely similar. You even seem to complete each other's sentences. Yes…you, indeed, must have been together for a very long time."

And he smiled at them.

The Carters smiled back.

Ten minutes later, Hossam Mahfouz brought his horse and carriage to a slow halt near a dock alongside the Nile. An older man and a young assistant, probably his son or grandson, approached the carriage and the younger of the two petted the horse on his muzzle.

"Masa el Khair, Baako...ehna mestanienak *Good evening, Baako...we are waiting for you!*"

Baako smiled and jumped down from the carriage.

The three Americans were quick to hop down and were introduced to the two men.

Before getting out of the carriage, Adam Carter leaned into his sister and whispered softly in her ear.

"We had better watch our Ps and Qs this evening, Addy. That Reckling chap, or Reckless, or whatever his name is made some awfully fast observations. Made me a wee bit uncomfortable, it did."

"Me, too, dear. Me, too. I don't like it," she answered sotto voce. "I don't like *him.*"

"Perhaps nothing will come of it," Adam said, shaking his head.

Adeline Carter wasn't so sure. The Carters got out of the carriage and headed to the boat.

Marcus Darke smiled at his friend, Reckless, and whispered into his ear after the Carters had passed them.

"You're always analyzing, aren't you? You seemed to pick up on the poor old Carters' quirks in a hurry."

"I'm always listening and looking for the lie, Marcus. I can't help it. It's what I do. It's what I'm best at. I can't turn it off. The Carters might be old, but they're certainly not poor. I think perhaps there's something else going on here."

"You're on vacation, you know. You're not working a case for any law firm."

"Yeah, yeah...I know. And *you're* supposed to be doing research over here. I thought I could help. Can you switch off *your* talent? *Your* ability? Aren't your creative juices spinning all the time?"

"You're right, Reckless. I'm always running scenes and scenarios through my mind. My characters even talk to me in my sleep. So you're suggesting that I'm supposed to write another Darke Mystery about two doddering old English folks, probably on their last legs? Two nefarious, murderous octogenarians. What, Miss Marple kills Hercule Poirot, or something like that? And buries his body under the Sphinx?"

Sebastian laughed and shrugged his shoulders.

"You never know! There could be a lot of scary things happening out there in the desert."

"It wouldn't sell," Marcus replied.

"Hey, you two," Valencia called to them, "quit your lollygagging and get your sorry butts down here on the boat…or we'll go without you."

Baako chuckled. He had no idea what lollygagging meant but it sure sounded funny.

Marcus and Sebastian hopped down into the felucca just as it was pulling away from the dock. The gentle evening breeze caught the large single sail and the craft headed out onto the wide Nile, drifting lazily out into the early evening glow. The sun was setting and the call to evening prayers could be heard from minarets, distant and near.

It was a pleasant hour with this group, with Baako pointing out various sites along the riverbanks. Valencia was clicking away with her camera, photographing the sights as well as her fellow passengers. The Carter twins were very cautious with what they said and did, actually enjoying the leisurely cruise.

Hossam Mahfouz was waiting for them on the dock when the felucca slowly drifted back.

"And now, my new friends," Baako said, "you will be in for a special evening of food you probably never thought you would ever eat. And, no doubt, you five will be the only tourists in the place."

Twenty minutes later they all disembarked from the carriage once again and gazed at a restaurant in the working class neighborhood of Rod el-Farag. The aromas drifting out from the establishment, Sobhy Kabar, were certainly tantalizing.

The three Americans looked enthused. The Carter twins looked apprehensive. It was now dark and the narrow street was filled with dozens of men in galabiyas, hardly any women, street vendors, donkey carts, and even one man leading a camel.

Hossam Mafouz's horse pricked his ears and nickered loudly when he saw the camel.

"Is it safe here?" Adeline Carter asked as she cautiously looked around the neighborhood and back up at the restaurant whose name was in Arabic.

"For whom?" Baako asked as he chuckled. "Us or them?"

He ushered them inside and was instantly greeted by a rotund man just inside the door. He had very dark skin, a black beard, was wearing a flowing deep burgundy galabiya and a black fez. His smile widened as he saw Baako Mustafa.

"Salam 'alaykum, Baako, my friend…welcome!" the man exclaimed loudly, giving him a warm hug and kissing him on both cheeks. Baako returned the gesture.

The place was packed with noisy, loud, hungry patrons at every table, and somewhere in the dark shadows two men were playing an Egyptian Oud (a type of guitar) and a Darbuka tabla doumbek (a tall fan drum). The greeter swiftly led the group to a very private room at the back of the restaurant. They were seated at a large, round table.

In Arabic, Baako told the server, who had appeared quickly, to bring platters for everyone and then ordered for the table.

"Bring enough for everyone to share. I want them to taste what we Egyptians love about our cuisine."

To begin with, he ordered molokhia (a rich, green stew with small pieces of rabbit meat); followed by mombar (sausage casings made from goat intestines stuffed with spiced herb rice); hamam mahshi (fried pigeon stuffed with cracked wheat and gizzards); and finally koshary (rice, lentils, macaroni, chickpeas, tomatoes, and vinegar). Before he had finished ordering a large bowl had been placed in the center of the table with a huge serving spoon leaning on its edge. The bowl was filled with Torshi (pickled vegetables with a combination of cucumber, cauliflower, carrots, and peppers).

"And the usual for you, Baako?" asked the server.

Baako smiled and nodded.

"Mashy," he replied. "*Okay.*"

As each dish was presented to the table, Baako explained what it was. The American trio seemed delighted…Marcus Darke furiously started taking notes, asking Baako for the spellings, because he knew his readers loved *all* the details he put into his books, no matter how minor or trivial. Valencia took photo after photo. Sebastian Reckling didn't hesitate to start dishing up his plate. The Carter twins looked at one another and shrugged. Baako laughed when he saw their expressions.

"Unless you have any strange allergies, you should be perfectly safe with this food. Just don't drink the water. I'll have them bring several unopened bottles of mineral water. Some with gas, some without."

"Why are *you* not eating, lad?" Adam Carter asked of Baako.

No sooner had he spoken than a server placed a large platter in front of Baako. A steaming slab of meat atop a mound of rice.

Baako smiled, leaned over the platter and took a deep whiff.

"This is an acquired taste," he said as he began to carve the meat, "and one of my favorites. You're welcome to take a bite if you'd like. Slow-roasted camel liver."

Marcus Darke wrote that down...Valencia declined to take a photo. No one requested a sample taste.

Food was passed around and soon the group was enthralled by the new tastes and textures. The table talk, at first, began as comments on the cuisine but soon the group began to warm up with each other and the questions began flowing.

"The three of you are here on holiday," Adam Carter addressed the three Americans. "We started this discussion earlier. Do you travel together often?"

Marcus Darke chuckled.

"Maybe you don't know who I am and haven't read any of my books, but I write murder mysteries and I always research the locales of my novels beforehand. I like to give my readers a true sense of place. Valencia helps with the technical research...and my friend here, Reckless, assists in another way."

Adeline Carter's ears perked up when Marcus mentioned what he does.

"Murder mysteries!" Adeline exclaimed loudly. "I do so love them. Dear Agatha Christie is my favorite. Wait," she said with a quizzical look on her face. "Marcus Darke. Marcus Darke. Yes! I think I *did* read one of yours. Something about dancing with the devil, wasn't it?"

Marcus blushed.

"That was my very first one, yes. That's the one that set me going. Perhaps you saw the film version? It was quite good, if I do say myself, even if the screenwriters changed it around a bit and changed the ending."

"No," answered Adam with a huff and a sniff, "we never go to the cinema. Live theater, yes, but the crass cinema...never."

"Another of my favorite authors...British, of course," Adeline quickly interjected, "is Devon Stone. Perhaps you've heard of him?"

"As a matter of fact," answered Marcus, "I *have*. I actually went to one of his book signings back in the States. Delightful man. So personable. I read only one of his so far, *A Taste For Murder*. I believe that may have been his very first. Quite funny in places."

"Oh", gushed Adeline, "my favorite is *The Fallen*. Delicious tale of revenge murders. Simply *delicious*! I love those."

Sebastian Reckling perked up. He finished chewing what he had in his mouth and put down his fork.

"Delicious is a strange term to use, don't you think?" he asked Adeline. "I don't remember that adjective being applied to murders…unless you're a cannibal, that is."

That made everyone laugh.

The Carter twins looked at each other and smiled.

"No, no, no, my dear," laughed Adeline, "no cannibal tendencies here, but I just *love* the reasoning behind all those revenge killings. I actually sympathize with the killers at times. Especially in *The Fallen*, although the poor thing met her demise at the end. I hated that part."

Sebastian Reckling sat back and stared at Adeline Carter for a brief moment.

"Are *you* harboring any secret tendencies for revenge killings, Mrs. Carter?"

Adeline Carter clutched her ample bosom and shook her head, wattle wagging beneath her chin, and laughed raucously.

"Oh, my *dear*…if I answered *that* question it wouldn't be a secret any longer, would it?"

And everyone laughed once again.

Intriguing answer, Sebastian thought. *Intriguing and noncommittal.*

"Well then, Marcus," Adeline continued, "you have obviously committed several murders, albeit fictional, so you must be an expert on the subject. Is there such a thing as a perfect murder?"

"You know, I have been asked that question several times at book signings and I've addressed it even more recently with Baako," Marcus answered. "Murders, basically, are spontaneous, reckless, and stupid actions. Rage, jealousy…emotional outbursts…money. Family arguments about politics at Thanksgiving gatherings. Money and murder almost always seem to go hand in hand. But, as I always say, I believe that a perfect murder takes time. It must be carefully plotted. All the details carefully worked out. It's about preparation and patience. By the same token, a perfect murder takes time to solve. But still *not* infallible. Two examples…

one fact, one fiction. The so-called *crime of the century*, way back in 1924. Two young college students, who thought they each had superior intellect, decided to commit the perfect crime. The perfect murder. Leopold and Loeb kidnapped and murdered a 14-year-old boy. They spent seven months planning absolutely everything, from the abduction to the disposal of the body. Oh, Mrs. Carter, they were very, very clever young men. They were done in, however, by a very special pair of prescription eyeglasses dropped carelessly by Leopold at the place where the body was found. But then again, look at what Patricia Highsmith wrote about in *Strangers On A Train*, for example. Perhaps you have read *that* one. The murders were supposedly carefully, ingeniously planned. No motive for each of the victims to be murdered. Two murders. Two victims. Each victim unknown to, or by the killer. Of course, in this case, the murderers were uncovered. By their own guilt, at that."

"Interesting," said Adeline Carter. "And if one should harbor no guilt whatsoever? What then, Mr. Mystery Writer…what then?"

"So then," Marcus responded, "I went a long way all around the block to answer your question, Adeline, but no, there is no such a thing as a perfect murder."

"Surely you can't be serious?" Adeline asked, cocking her head.

"What? You don't believe me?" Marcus laughed.

Adeline threw up her hands and shrugged her shoulders.

"Why should I believe you when you spend your entire life making things up?"

"Ha!" hooted Adam Carter, clapping his hands. "Well played, Addy… well played!"

"And what if," Adeline continued, "the crime goes undetected? What then? Wouldn't *that* be perfect?"

Marcus Darke wrinkled his brow.

"Depends upon the crime, of course," he responded, "but I doubt that *murders* go undetected."

Sebastian Reckling's professional instincts and intuition had kicked into high gear. But for what purpose? And to what end? What was he supposed to do about it? What was it about these two old, seemingly gentle people…the woman, especially? He was distressed because he had never felt this way about anyone so quickly before.

The meal continued and the conversation returned to their itineraries while in Egypt.

"Tomorrow will be a museum day for you three," Baako said, referring to the Americans. "The Cairo Museum is filled with wonders that will give you, Marcus, a lot of solid reference material for your book. Maybe you're planning on a murder there? Who knows?"

"Time will tell, Baako…time will tell. And then, on the following day, we shall all head down to Upper Egypt?"

"Wait," said Sebastian, "you said *down* to Upper Egypt? Down is up here?"

Baako and Marcus laughed.

"I know what that means, Baako. Don't pay attention to Reckless here."

"Yes, Sebastian," Baako said, "we're talking about elevation in this case. Upper Egypt, in the south, is at a higher elevation than Lower Egypt is here in the north. So, logically, here we can say we are going up south and down north."

Again the entire table laughed.

"And tomorrow morning" Adam Carter said, "we shall be taking the train up to Alexandria…but down north," and he winked. "Perhaps our paths may cross again at some time."

The exotic meal finished, they all headed back into the night. Hossam Mahfouz and his horse were patiently waiting out side, although it seemed that both of them had fallen asleep.

"It's too bad that Manal couldn't have joined us this evening," Valencia said. "She missed out on an enjoyable feast and some interesting conversation, that's for sure!"

Manal Khalifa had been very concerned and distressed. At 5:45 earlier that evening her father had called her at the hotel, something he never does, and told her to come home as soon as possible. Something was wrong. Something serious. She waited until she had sent her five guests out for the evening with Baako Mustafa and then headed for home.

When she entered the house, her mother was seated on the large sofa in the living room. She looked distraught and was crying. Her father wasn't seen, but there was a strange man sitting on a chair facing her mother. He appeared to be in his early forties with closely cropped dark curly hair, he had a mustache, and friendly, dark eyes. He smiled at her. A moment later her father entered the room carrying a copper tray with four glasses of tea. Always a polite host. He had obviously expected Manal to arrive home momentarily. Her father offered the tray to the man, who smiled and lifted one of the glasses.

"Masa' al-khair, my dear Manal," her father said, offering the tray to her. She declined.

She looked toward her mother who was gently wiping her eyes.

"Ma al-khatb, Baba?" Manal asked. "What's wrong, father?"

"Manal," her father said as he introduced the unfamiliar man. "This is Inspector Ahmed Mohammadi.

The man rose and bowed slightly toward Manal.

Manal's heart was racing *Inspector? What's happening here?* she was thinking.

"Your brother Aharon is missing," her father replied. "And has been for a week. We just found out about it."

Manal was confused. Aharon was the brother with a wife, children, and three secret mistresses.

"Just found out about it *now?* Why? Why just now?" She asked.

"Evidently," the inspector finally saying something, "he severely beat his wife and terrified his children. His wife finally notified the police when he failed to return home for the past week. She had been too ashamed to admit what had happened. Your parents are in a state of shock. They cannot believe that their son...your brother...could ever be violent. I'm sorry to say, but they are of the opinion that your brother's wife is lying. They are convinced that your brother has actually been killed by his wife."

Manal held her breath, but was silent. She shook her head.

The inspector noticed the hesitation.

"Is there something that you can tell me, Manal, that could shed some light onto this situation?"

"This is a private matter, Inspector," she answered.

"No. No, it's not. Now I'm afraid it's a police matter. A man is missing. A woman has been beaten, supposedly, and a couple of young children are too afraid to even speak. He has neither shown up at his place of employment nor called in to say why."

Manal looked back and forth at her parents. They were confused. They were upset, to say the least.

"Can we step outside for a moment, sir?" Manal asked. "I'm feeling faint and need a bit of air."

Inspector Mohammadi knew exactly what she was doing.

"Of course, young lady. I shall come with you in case you may, indeed, faint."

Manal excused herself from her parents and she stepped out onto a small, latticed balcony at the front of the house, followed by the Inspector.

"You know something about your brother that your parents do not, is that correct, Manal?"

Manal Khalifa couldn't help the tears that now streaked down her cheeks.

"Yes, I do, Inspector. You are correct. My siblings and I have been taught to be honest and faithful. I love my brother in a way…but I fear him as well. We are not very close. Haven't been for a few years. Yes, he's married. To a beautiful and loving wife. His children adore him. Well, *adored* him. My parents would die of shame if they knew what I know. Against our teachings, Aharon has taken three mistresses. I think he may also be into bango…or hashish. No one knows but me. And he has threatened me…*strongly*…if I should ever reveal his secret life."

Inspector Ahmed Mohammadi shook his head, inhaled deeply, exhaled just as deeply and looked out into the middle-distance.

"That complicates the matter, then, doesn't it, Manal?" he asked.

Bango and hashish, both of them forms of cannabis, are the main drugs of abuse in Egypt, mainly among the male population between the ages of twenty and thirty years of age.

Three days earlier, Aharon Khalifa, Manal's brother, awoke with a horrendous headache. He felt nauseated. His right eye was painful and swollen shut. He licked his dry lips and tasted blood. The room was very dark, smelled musty, and he had no idea where he was. He tried to move but he could not. Obviously he was lying on a bed of some kind, but he didn't know whose. His arms and legs were tied, spread-eagled, to the bedposts. Suddenly he realized that he was naked. Who had stripped him of his clothing? And why?

Someone spoke and Aharon jolted. His body flew into a panic as he struggled against the ropes that held his arms and legs. He had recognized the voice.

It was the voice of his wife's oldest brother.

Although his exploratory journey in Egypt had barely just begun, Marcus Darke would soon discover that he probably had enough material already to fill his next murder mystery. Possibly two. But more was yet to come. He just needed to pay attention.

PART TWO

Book of the Dead

*The educated differ from the uneducated as much
as the living differ from the dead.*
Aristotle

13

Swaffham, England

After examining her sewing room thoroughly, Detective Chief Inspector Weldon Atherstone had deduced that the deceased, Eudora Smythe, was, indeed, a decorator. On her desk he had found a large ledger with clients names, addresses, and telephone numbers. A smaller book with listings of her current projects in the works lay on top of the ledger. One such project's due date was for two days following her death. He took the books back to his office.

Atherstone picked up the phone on his desk and asked the operator to reach the number of that client...the client who would *not* be receiving her finished work, whatever it might have been.

After five rings the telephone was answered and the officer introduced himself. He could hear soft classical music playing in the background.

"I'm sorry to bother you, Miss Thorndycroft, but..."

"It's *Mrs.* Thorndycroft, Inspector," came the abrupt reply and Weldon Atherstone immediately recognized that the woman spoke with a strong northern dialect. "Although I'm a widow now. Glad that fookin' old blighter is gone, if you ask me!"

The Inspector rolled his eyes. A merry widow, indeed.

"My apologies," he replied. "I am calling in regard to the untimely demise of Eudora Smythe and..."

Again, he was abruptly interrupted.

"Christ almighty! When I read about that in the press I felt as though I had been run over by a bus," she exclaimed, pronouncing *bus* as *boose*. "I loved that dear, talented woman. She has practically redecorated my entire flat."

"Again, my apologies for the intrusion *Mrs.* Thorndycroft, but if I may ask a few questions about her it might help in my investigation. The press has only alluded to it, but I'm fairly certain her death was not by natural causes."

"I thought the same, Chief Inspector...the very same, if you ask me."

"I'm going through her client listing, and will contact a few more... but yours was the project that was due to be completed the closest to her... well,...her departure. The interesting thing is, though, there is a name that is *not* on her client listing. A name that she had written...or rather, had started to write on a piece of paper in her last moments evidently."

"And that name would be?"

"Do you happen to know anyone by the name of Adeline?"

There was a very audible gasp at the other end of the line.

"Really? I never met the woman, Inspector, but Eudora spoke of her often."

"In what manner?"

"As I said, I never met her...never even saw her...so it's only hearsay, if you ask me. Adeline Carter and her twin brother Adam live across the street from Eudora. They seem to have a reputation around town for being sweet, gentle older folks. Somewhat befuddled, I suppose. I believe they might be in their early eighties or there about. Well! Eudora says it's all a *big* act, if you ask me. The two old fogies ain't nearly as sweet as they appear. Don't ask me how Eudora came about that. She never elaborated but she was becoming a bit frightened by them, if you ask me. Eudora was a very good judge of character. She had a dear sweet old cat that was practically blind but would wander into the Carter's yard at times and she saw Adam throw rocks at the poor old puss. From what I'm told, something's not right with them two people, Inspector, if you ask me."

Cairo, Egypt...10 A.M.

Baako Mustafa was waiting in the lobby of the Mena House when Marcus and Valencia appeared.

"Reckless will join us in a minute or so," Valencia said. "I think he wanted to stop in and say good morning to Manal and tell her what an enjoyable evening she missed."

Two minutes late Sebastian Reckling walked up to them and shrugged his shoulders.

"Manal isn't in," he said. "Her assistant is handling the job this morning. Evidently there was a family issue that needed addressing. Must be serious."

Shortly after 10 A.M., Adeline and Adam Carter boarded the train at Cairo's Ramses Train Station for the nearly four-hour ride to Alexandria, on the Mediterranean coast.

Twenty minutes into the ride Adeline sat comfortably reading *Hickory, Dickory, Dock*, the very latest Agatha Christie novel. She chuckled out loud to herself because the plot, with her favorite detective Hercule Poirot, was about an outbreak of kleptomania at a student hostel. Adam had gone to the toilet.

A few moments later, Adam Carter returned to sit down again beside his sister.

"Look what I found, dear," he said as he held out his hand cautiously, lowering it so no one else could see. It was a very delicate Cartier watch with a thin gold strap.

"Oh, isn't that simply beautiful! Lovely. And, uh...just *where* did you find it, dear?"

"On the wrist of a sweet young thing I bumped into on the way back from the loo. Here. Better put it into your purse quickly."

Three hours later when they disembarked at Misr Train Station in Alexandria, and thanks to Adam's trip to the lounge car for some tea, Adeline had added in her oversized purse two men's wristwatches (one of which was a vintage Blancpain), a wallet with a fair amount of Egyptian pounds, and a sterling silver cigarette lighter.

It was beginning to rain lightly as they casually walked along the platform heading into the station. They passed a small group of passengers arguing with a conductor and a police officer. A young woman was sobbing.

"See what you caused, you bad boy?" Adeline chuckled.

Adam smirked, cocking his head, as they continued on with nary a glance back at the agitated group.

Alexandria, Egypt

Founded in 331 B.C. by Alexander the Great, at its earliest it was that largest city in the world. Rome, Italy, later on, toppled that claim although Rome had neither the architectural grandeur nor the exemplary culture. Alexandria was a glistening jewel on an equally glistening Mediterranean. At the time of Cleopatra's reign, 51 – 30 B.C., it was also the fashion capital of the world...Cleopatra being a beloved queen as well as quite the fashionista. She could well afford to be. She was the wealthiest woman in the world. And the most influential. Alexandria is where she had her palace. Unfortunately, after a fifth-century earthquake Cleopatra's palace slid into the Mediterranean to be lost forever.

January often brings sudden wet, blustery storms off the Mediterranean Sea and today was one of those days.

The Carter twins, as impressed as they were with the old elegance of the palace-like train station, were aghast at the weather when they approached the exit.

"Looks like we left the warmth and sun of Cairo behind us, dear," muttered Adeline. "We won't be doing any exploring outside today, will we?"

A doddering elderly couple seemed to be easy prey for a crafty taxicab driver who had been waiting for a fare just outside the station. He saw them standing just inside the station's doorway and he could tell they were very obviously *not* Egyptian.

"Welcome, welcome," he called out to them, waving his arms. "English, yes? Let me help you! Tell me where you go and I will take."

He reached to lift their suitcases but Adam stopped him.

"We need to go to Le Metropole Hotel. Do you know where that is?"

"Ya, ya...everyone knows Metropole. Beautiful hotel. I take you."

Again, he reached for their luggage and, again, Adam stopped him.

"And how far is it?" Adeline asked.

"Oh...perhaps...umm...thirty minutes in all this traffic and bad weather. No worries. I give you good price."

Adam stared the man square in the face.

"Just because we're old doesn't mean we're fools, you rascal. Trying to cheat us, are you, you old sot. You won't get one piaster from us. I happen to know that the hotel is just a short walk from here. We shall see if the rain soon abates and then we shall get there via shank's mare."

The taxicab driver had no idea what that meant.

"So get lost, you nasty little man," said Adeline with a wave of her hand. "Be gone!"

The cabbie muttered something under his breath as he turned and walked away, but the Carters paid no attention.

A few minutes later a group of other tourists, again, obviously not Egyptian or Middle Eastern, emerged from the train station. The cab driver hurried to accost *them* now.

"Welcome, welcome," he called out to them, waving his arms "English, yes?"

"American," answered one of the men.

"Oh...I like Ike!" answered the cabbie. "Where you go? I will take. Good price."

As quickly as the storm had swept in from the sea, it soon was gone and the skies cleared. The sun shone brightly as the clouds slowly drifted away.

The Carters gathered their luggage and headed to their hotel two blocks away. Adam was a bit more agile than his sister, who came huffing and puffing close behind. Cars, with horns honking, whizzed past them as they walked. The beautiful azure Mediterranean was just across the street from their destination.

The Metropole Hotel was an interesting sight. Old, classic and very pink. It looked like a big six-story birthday cake with strawberry frosting.

The Carters were soon shown to their room that had a beautiful little balcony overlooking a now-sparkling Mediterranean. They were both impressed.

Two hours after checking in, their guide, arranged for them by Thomas Cook & Son, called their room from the lobby.

Tirian Trevor, a jovial expatriate Welshman, would soon give Adeline some interesting...and deadly information.

Meanwhile, Baako Mustafa was guiding the three Americans through the magnificent Cairo Museum. The Americans had stood agape as they entered the massive salmon-pink colored building. Large galleries stretched out before them and to either side. The ceilings were vaulted overhead, with a series of large arches stretched across the second floor above them.

The young Egyptologist described statuary, papyri, and various artifacts found in countless tombs in vivid detail. They were overwhelmed.

"What in the *hell* is that?" Sebastian Reckling asked Baako as he stared at a framed piece of tattered papyrus.

They had all been strolling through the vast hallways of the museum for several hours, with Baako being nonstop talking with his history lesson, when they came upon this unique piece on the museum's upper floor.

Baako laughed and shook his head.

"You will see a *lot* of papyri while you're in our glorious country," he said, "but none as strange as this particular one."

The artwork in question was a rare example of Egyptian satire. Yes, the ancient Egyptians had an acute sense of humor. No human forms were in this piece; instead, cats were waiting on and serving mice with beverages.

"It's totally symbolic, of course," Baako said as he pointed to the various animal figures, "and intended as satire. This was done during a particular period of weakness in our history. The cats, here, represent Egyptians and the mice and rats represent foreigners who have become the center of power at that time."

Baako was thinking how ironic that this piece of artwork drew their attention. Egyptians were presently feeling oppressed by the long British occupation. He knew there was unrest in the streets and he feared that the politics could turn nasty at any moment. He hoped, however, not while his clients were still in the country. The warning, earlier in the week, from his friend Hossam Mahfouz had stayed in his mind.

Cameras were not permitted in the museum, so Marcus Darke was writing as fast as he could in his large notebook and scribbling a hasty sketch of the papyrus.

Baako led them to another elaborate, very colorful papyrus.

"This represents a very serious aspect of an Egyptian's life...well, actually, his or her death," he said. "This is but a very small part of the Book of the Dead. The rest is in some British museum. But what this depicts is that after one dies, the jackal-headed god Anubis leads the deceased into the presence of Osiris. There, the dead person will recite a text known as the Forty-two Negative Confessions, swearing that he committed no sins throughout his life. Then the dead person's heart is weighed on a balancing scale. His heart on one side, a feather on the other. If the scale balances, or the heart is lighter than the feather, then that means that the deceased has led a good, virtuous life. He would then be taken to meet Osiris and they would take their place in the pleasurable afterlife. If, however, the heart is heavier than the feather a fearsome beast called Ammit the Devourer would eat it and put the dead person's afterlife to an early and rather unpleasant end."

Sebastian Reckling arched his eyebrows.

"You know," Marcus said, after some thought, "I notice that all the various forms of artwork that we've seen today cover centuries in Egyptian history. *Thousands* of years. But the style of the artwork doesn't seem to change at all. Maybe just a little, but not very much at all. Elsewhere in the world we've had such art movements as Impressionism, Cubism, Surrealism, and now, for Pete's sake, we have Pop Art coming at us. The Egyptian art *all* looks like it was done by the same artist, although that's impossible."

"You must be reading my mind," Valencia interjected. "I noticed the exact same thing. Why doesn't the style ever change?"

Baako nodded his head.

"And you shall notice that exact same thing when we visit the temples along the Nile. The carvings and the friezes. That is an excellent question. One, surprisingly, I am asked rarely. The *simple* answer is that our Egyptian artists were not exposed to outward influences. They did not see artwork from other cultures. Obviously they had never traveled out of our country. But the more *complex* answer is that Egyptian artwork is closely linked to religious belief and the afterlife. That required specific representations of gods and goddesses. Artists were bound by strict rules, probably set by the pharaohs, ensuring consistency. Cosmic order, in other words. The artists had to follow these rules and not express their own particular styles. The consistent look was intentional throughout the centuries."

Baako had saved the best part of his tour through the museum for last. One he knew would thoroughly impress the trio and leave them speechless.

He ushered them into the most guarded display room in the museum. The treasures retrieved from the tomb of Tutankhamun. They all gazed at numerous statues in gold, stone, or ivory; a golden throne with lion's feet; numerous pieces of jewelry…and then the one thing that made them gasp with amazement. The young king's funerary mask. It was simply stunning. Wearing a bright shining gold headcloth alternating dark blue, almost black, horizontal stripes around the youthful features of the king, with his large eyes of translucent quartz dramatically outlined in black to mimic khol. On his brow the two figures of a vulture and a hooded cobra, representing Upper Egypt and Lower Egypt, stared at the viewers.

"That's twenty-two pounds of solid gold," Baako said as he pointed to the mask.

The three Americans were stunned into total silence as they stared at the magnificent piece as they slowly strolled around and around the glass case in which it was propped. On the back of the mask, what would have rested on the king's shoulders, a protective spell was inscribed in hieroglyphics. The spell had first appeared five hundred years before the young king had been born and was from the Book of the Dead. Baako explained exactly what it was to the trio, who were still staring agape at the magnificent piece.

"That particular spell is from Chapter 151 of the Book of the Dead. It protects the various limbs on Tutankhamun's body as he moves into the underworld."

"Okay," Marcus Darke said, leaning in closer to look at the inscription, "A spell, huh? So what about the dreaded curse of the mummy we've heard about? Obviously Tut, here, had some protection in the afterlife for a reason."

Baako Mustafa simply rolled his eyes.

"Superstition and rumors, nothing more," he responded. "Yes, one of Howard Carter's partners in the excavation, Lord Carnarvon, died shortly after the tomb's opening, but mere happenstance. He was simply bitten by a mosquito. While shaving with a straight-edged razor the next day, he nicked the bite causing it to become infected. He had never been a strong person anyway, health-wise, so a fever set in resulting in pneumonia. He died. Nothing more than that. End of curse."

But there *was* more than that.

Baako failed to mention the other weird occurrences surrounding the opening of the tomb. On the day that the tomb was opened, a cobra swallowed Carter's pet canary that he always had with him. At the precise moment of Carnarvon's death the lights of Cairo inexplicably went out; while at *that* exact same time in England, Carnarvon's beloved terrier, Susie, howled and dropped dead.

Of the twenty-six people who had been present at the opening of the tomb, six were dead within the next few years, a few from weird circumstances.

"I don't suppose," Sebastian Reckling said as he backed away from the case that held the mask, "that any of these mummies you showed us around this place wake up at night and stroll aimlessly through the corridors?"

"Reckless," Valencia laughingly said as she shook her head, "you're an idiot!"

"None of the nighttime guards here have died of fright...yet. But you never know!" Baako laughed in response.

His tour of the Cairo Museum was winding down and they all headed out into the brilliant early afternoon sunlight.

"Our itinerary will now take us out of Cairo for the next few days. My friend Hossam will meet you at the hotel with his carriage at 5:30 and take you to the station. I shall meet you there. Be wary, it will be very crowded and noisy, but I will find you. We're able to take the overnight train to Luxor from the Giza train station," Baako told the three Americans, "and so we won't have to hassle with all the Cairo traffic and congestion at that time. They might call it First Class, but I wouldn't let that go to your heads. I have booked two sleeper compartments for us. Marcus and Valencia, obviously you will be in one and, if you have no objections Sebastian, you and I shall be in the one next to them."

Sebastian Reckling thought about that for a moment.

"I have no idea how you guys sleep over here," he said, "I just won't have to see you naked, will I?"

"Remember what I said a few minutes ago?" Valencia said, again shaking her head. "You're an idiot!"

Baako Mustafa shook *his* head and laughed.

"I have been asked many, *many* questions throughout my short years as a tour guide. *That* one, my friend, is the most outlandish. But to put your very strange mind at ease, at home I *do*, indeed, sleep in the nude within my comfortable sheets. However, I have ridden this overnight train countless times and their bedding is rough and scratchy. Modesty and my comfort will dictate that I wear some form of attire while sleeping. Therefore, you will not have the pleasure to gaze upon my splendid body."

Marcus and Valencia could not stop laughing.

"Just a note of caution, Baako," Marcus said while still laughing, "You might want to sleep with one eye open. Reckless has a notorious reputation. He'll fuck anything that moves. Especially after dark."

"Well, then," Baako responded without hesitation, "I shall sleep with my scimitar beneath my pillow just in case. I have neutered horses before."

Sebastian Reckling made an obscene gesture with his middle finger... and they all laughed.

14

Alexandria, Egypt

Tirian Trevor was slowly leading Adeline and Adam Carter down a deep rough stone circular stairwell into the Catacombs of Kom el-Shoqafa. The stairwell lead down into the tombs that had been tunneled into the bedrock during the age of the Antoine emperors during the second century. There didn't appear to be any other tourist walking down here. It was dank, and quiet. Adeline was becoming a bit uneasy as she glanced all around.

The subject of Cleopatra, as a result, would come up quite by accident.

"This is a very uncomfortable place," Adeline said. "I don't like creepy surroundings like this."

Adam and their Welsh guide chuckled.

"Nothing to fear, my dear woman," said Tirian Trevor, "nothing to fear. Yes, it's where dead things have been found, but not recently. And I don't believe that they're still around."

"Any snakes, down here? And spiders? I have a deathly fear of snakes," Adeline said with a shudder.

"Again, my dear, I've never seen any snakes down here. Spiders? Oh, yes. But snakes? Never."

They walked a little bit further. A thought struck Adam.

"Speaking of snakes, where do you suppose that Cleopatra got *that* famous snake of hers…you know, the one that she committed suicide with. An asp, wasn't it?"

"Well," Tirian said, stopping in his tracks. "I have a bit of startling news for you both in that regard. That story is pure fabrication, I'm afraid to tell you. More myth than fact, it is. Certainly good for dramatists, but rebuffed by historians."

"What do you mean?" asked a shocked Adeline. "You're telling us that's a lie? What we have all learned in school about that?"

The guide sighed deeply.

"A story, for sure, not a lie. There is a difference, is there not? To be honest, it seems very unlikely that a simple but deadly snake could have killed dear, sweet *devious* Cleopatra. No. Not at all. First of all, two other handmaidens of hers died along side of her. You might convince a snake to bite one person…Cleopatra perhaps…but to then turn around and bite two others and then slither away? Unlikely. No, the truth is that Cleopatra was a very smart, as well as murderous, soul. Oh, she *was* a merry murderess that one was. Did you know that, not unlike the current author Agatha Christie in *your* country, Cleopatra was an expert on poisons?"

Adeline Carter perked up. Forgetting her unease at the locale.

"Really, now?" she exclaimed.

"Oh, yes, my dear. I'm not kidding you. She experimented a lot with them. Killing many unsuspecting sots, including siblings. The truth is that Cleopatra probably poisoned her two handmaidens then drank the poison herself."

"And just what *was* this poison?" Adeline asked, as Adam stood back with a smirk on his face.

"Perhaps it was one of her favorites," Tirian Trevor answered. "It could have been a combination of opium, wolfsbane, and hemlock. Painless and swift."

"How interesting," Adeline said. "How *very* interesting."

"Baako wasn't kidding, was he?" Valencia said, as the three Americans were lost amongst the throngs of noisy Egyptians at the train station later that evening. They could hardly move, it was so crowded.

Five minutes later it got even noisier as the train slowly pulled into the station. Valencia let out a little startled shriek as the train blew its shrill, loud whistle.

They heard someone call out Baako's name. Then another.

Baako Mustafa finally appeared weaving his way through the crowd as he greeted several others around him with smiles and handshakes.

"Jeepers, You must be the most popular guy in Egypt," Valencia said as their guide strolled up to them.

Baako shrugged his shoulders.

"What can I say?" Baako answered. "I get around. Here, this is our carriage," as he gestured for the group to get on one of the train cars. Marcus, you and your wife are in compartment number eleven. Sebastian, you and I will be in twelve. Be prepared for First Class, Egyptian railway style." And he laughed.

A smiling attendant greeted them as they stepped onboard and escorted them down the narrow passageway to their respective compartments. Despite what Baako had said sarcastically, Marcus and Valencia found the compartment very accommodating and pleasant, if somewhat old and worn. The compartment consisted of two large seats, which would be turned into a bed at night, and then one bed above which forms the second bunk. There was a ladder to get up to the top bunk. They would later find that the beds had a thin, but decent mattress, with a sheet, a thin blanket and a not-too fluffy pillow.

There was a small sink with an equally small mirror above it. The three Americans were very well travelled and always carried light, smartly packed luggage, which was wise because the storage space for luggage in the compartment was limited, to say the least.

Between the lower seats there was a small tray, which would obviously serve as their meal tray when the porter served it. They would be served an evening meal as well as a breakfast prior to their arrival in Luxor.

Two toilet compartments, to be shared by the passengers, were on either end of each of the train's passenger cars.

The train scheduled departure time was 6:35 and precisely at 6:34 they all heard the train's whistle blow sharply. The engine slowly lurched forward and they were off...but not for long. A short stop at the congested Cairo station for more passengers and the train finally began its journey to Luxor, ten hours away, at 7:15.

Although Baako was quite familiar with the train, the others soon discovered that not only was it a very noisy ride, but a bumpy, jumpy one as well.

A half hour into their journey, a porter knocked on their compartment door serving them the dinner. It looked, smelled, and tasted much like airplane food…only a bit worse. Valencia wrinkled up her nose as she unwrapped the foil covering on her plate. Marcus laughed.

"Bon appetite!" he snickered. "Sorry, dear, I forgot to bring the wine."

In the next compartment, Baako ushered the porter in and spoke to him in Arabic and they both laughed.

After the trays of food were placed on the small table between the seats and the porter departed, Baako smiled at Sebastian.

"That was rude of me, I know, but I told the porter I was eager to see your expression when you see this…umm…first class meal."

Sebastian Recklin pulled back the foil on his meal and shrugged his shoulders.

"What the hell," he said, "I've eaten worse. Let's dig in!"

As the two men sat side-by-side eating their dinner, Baako thought about what Marcus Darke had said about the reputation of his traveling companion.

"I have no doubt Marcus may have been joking about your…hmmm… proclivity," Baako said. "I remember, then, that you are not currently married. You spoke of this to some degree when we were dining with the Carters."

Sebastian Reckling had to think long and hard before answering the Egyptian. He had learned in college about the psychological principle called the "Halo Effect". This is where one negative aspect of a person can overshadow all of their positive traits in the eyes of others. If one shares past mistakes too readily, one might be judged on those errors rather than seeing the full picture of who they are now.

"Yes, Baako," he began with a sigh, "I *have* been married. Twice for that matter. Both times mistakes, I'm sorry to say. Mistakes *I* made. All *my* mistakes. Careless, stupid mistakes. They came with regrets I now have. My nickname, Reckless, is justly deserved for various reasons, I suppose. But I don't usually talk about this with others who don't know me very well."

Baako shrugged his shoulders and continued eating without comment.

Sebastian sat quietly for a moment before speaking again. For some strange reason, all of a sudden he was feeling ashamed of himself and his past behaviors.

"He was joking and being very crude, of course, but…based on what my friend Marcus said about me fucking anything that moves, you're probably thinking that I lack some sort of moral compass, aren't you?"

"I do not judge," Baako answered, shrugging his shoulders again. "It serves me no purpose. And who am *I* to judge? Although, to be honest, several of the travelers I have guided around our glorious country have caused my eyebrows to raise and my head to shake in disbelief. Your moral compass, as you call it, might spin recklessly…no pun intended, but you must let your own conscience be *your* guide, my friend. Bear in mind, at some time you *will* be judged however. In your final journey to the afterlife will *your* heart be lighter than a feather?"

In that instant, Sebastian Reckling felt an unfamiliar heat of embarrassment surge through his body. He could feel it on his face.

"Baako, my friend, you might not believe this…or even *want* to believe this…but with those words of wisdom you have just changed my life."

They all had agreed earlier to meet in the train's lounge car following their meal. Marcus and Valencia were already there when Sebastian and Baako arrived. The Egyptian knew what to expect. The Americans did not. Everyone in the car was smoking. It was almost difficult to see from one end of the lounge to the other. Valencia nearly choked on the air.

The Americans had thought that perhaps an after dinner cocktail would be nice, but they were disappointed. Because of the Egyptian laws, no alcohol was being served at the bar, only tea, coffee, and various juices. There were snack cakes and biscuits available but none of them looked appealing.

Marcus, Valencia and Sebastian exchanged glances, not unnoticed by Baako.

"Shall we return to our compartments, then?" Baako asked with a slight chuckle.

All three of his companions nodded as one.

It was getting late. They were all tired. Baako and the three Americans left the smoke-filled lounge car and returned to their respective compartments, bidding each other good night as they entered, closing the doors behind them.

Baako, yawning, stood in the middle of their compartment, started to unbutton his shirt, and turned to look at Sebastian.

"Now then, are you a top or a bottom?" he asked.

"Excuse *me*?" Sebastian asked loudly, eyes suddenly wide open. He was taken aback by the question and momentarily alarmed, to say nothing of confused.

Baako Mustafa simply pointed to the upper bunk and then to the lower seat, which had now been converted into a bed by the porter when they were in the lounge car.

"Are you a top bunk or a bottom bunk?

"Jesus *Christ*, Baako! You had me scared for a minute."

Now it was Baako's turn to be confused.

Marcus was trying his best to be amorous but Valencia kept giggling. They were both in the mood for sex, finding the strange, exotic locale of a swiftly moving train enticing. But the small size of either bed…top or bottom…made it a bit uncomfortable and awkward. The loud rhythmic sound of the clickety-clack, clickety-clack, clickety-clack of the tracks and the jerkiness as the train barreled toward Luxor was more of a distraction than they had imagined.

Taking a few deep breaths between their respective giggles, they eventually fell into a more comfortable position, rocking gently with the movement of the train. Marcus soon found the perfect spot and the perfect rhythm.

At the exact moment when they reached a simultaneous climax, the train's whistle let out a loud, long blast. Marcus and Valencia collapsed in exhaustion and laughter.

15

Swaffham, England

The medical examiner had ascertained that the death of Eudora Smythe was by poison. Probably *not* of her own doing, obviously. Detective Chief Inspector Weldon Atherstone had already interviewed one client of the seamstress and had gotten a hint about a suspicious neighbor or two. The inspector approached the storefront, Harrison's Haberdashery, in hopes of discovering more about the personality of the deceased. He had found countless sales receipts for fabric and other notions from this shop, so he assumed Eudora Smythe had been a frequent customer.

A bell over the front door rang as the inspector entered the shop. The merchandise was neatly displayed, with tall, slanting shelves alongside one wall with a veritable rainbow of bolts of fabrics, segueing from solids into plaids and patterns. Rotating wire racks with patterns, shelves with various threads and yarns and cases of a variety of scissors were spaced throughout the shop.

Walter Harrison, owner of the shop, was a mousy little man of indeterminate age, standing no more than 5'5", and weighing no more than one hundred and twenty pounds. He had flaming red hair that was very obviously dyed, very pale flesh, and wore thin wire-rimmed glasses.

Harrison popped up from behind a wide cutting table to see who was entering. Not expecting to see a man, and such a good-looking man at that, he let out a wide smile.

"Well, good afternoon, sir," he said in a pleasant but squeaky thin voice, almost purring. "How may I help you?" And he batted his eyelashes.

"Are you the proprietor, sir?" Atherstone asked.

"I am, indeed." Another broad smile and eyelash batting. "My shop for the past twenty years or so. Are you a decorator?"

The inspector introduced himself and Walter's face deflated a bit.

"Oh," was his sole response.

"I am doing some investigating into the death of one of your customers...Eudora Smythe."

"Oh, goodness, gracious me," Walter Harrison replied, hands aflutter. "Terrible thing, that was but...oh, my. What a piece of work *she* was, you know what I'm saying?"

"I do *not* know. What do you mean by that, sir?"

"Don't get me wrong, she was a good customer, you know what I'm saying? But she was a paradox. Friendly one day...a mean old bitch...oh, sorry...a mean old lady another, you know what I'm saying?"

"In what way?"

"Oh, she loved all my textiles one day and hated them another, you know what I'm saying? And she *always* complained about my prices. Thought that she should get special discounts because of the amount of business she did here, you know what I'm saying? She tried to Jew me down every single time she shopped here. I felt like strangling her myself at times. Oh...wait...perhaps that wasn't the wisest of things to have said, you know what I'm saying?"

Detective Chief Inspector Atherstone took an instant dislike to this little man. He was offensive and his speech pattern swiftly became annoying.

"I don't like to gossip, mind you, and this is only hearsay, but Eudora loved to poke her nose into other peoples business, you know what I'm saying? She wanted to know what everyone was doing, where they were doing it, and how much it cost."

"Did she ever happen to mention anyone by the name of Adeline Carter?"

"Ooooh, she did, indeed, sir. She thought something was odd about that old woman and her brother, too. Twins, they are. An odd lot, you know what I'm saying?"

"Odd in what way, sir? Can you elaborate?"

"Actually, no. No, I can't, you know what I'm saying? I may have seen that old couple in town around here a few times, but never met them. You might want to ask some of the other shopkeepers around here, you know what I'm saying? Or at the bank. Eudora told me they went to the bank often. From what Eudora said they traveled a lot, you know what I'm saying?"

Detective Chief Inspector Weldon Atherstone concluded his interview with this obnoxious little man and his impression was that if the guy should sneeze hard enough he'd throw his back out...you know what I'm saying?

Ten minutes later, the Inspector entered the small Bank of Swaffham. It smelled old. Dark paneled walls, hunter green marble floors and two teller windows, one of which was being manned. He walked up to the window and was greeted by the friendly smile of Miss Wiggam. That's what the nameplate said on the white marble countertop. Miss Wiggam (*Estelle* Wiggam, as the inspector would learn) looked to be on the far side of fifty, silver hair done up in tiny, tight ringlets and wearing enough perfume to make a horse snort and recoil.

"Good morning, sir," she said with a toothy grin. "Beautiful day out there, isn't it?"

"Indeed it is, Miss Wiggam," the inspector replied, looking around and reaching into his suit jacket pocket. "I'm not here on bank business, however."

Miss Wiggam's smile disappeared, and she froze. *He's reaching into his pocket. Is this a robbery*, she thought quickly to herself. *Oh, dear God. Does he have a gun? I shall faint dead away!*

"It's a bit of police work, if you will," he said quickly, withdrawing a note pad and pen from his pocket. He knew what she must have been thinking. He then quickly introduced himself, showing his badge. He was glad that he was the only person other than the personnel in the bank.

"I'm investigating the death of Eudora Smythe," he said. And he could tell that Miss Wiggam relaxed a bit. At least she no longer looked as though she was about to faint.

"Oh, that poor, poor lady," Miss Wiggam said, clutching her hands to her chest. "She was one of the nicest, friendliest customers we had here. We all loved her."

Inspector Atherstone was momentarily silenced. And confused.

"I think you may have the Carter twins as bank customers as well, right?"

"Why, yes, Inspector, those sweet folks are customers here as well."

"Sweet?" he asked.

Miss Wiggam laughed.

"Why, yes...they are even sweeter than Eudora is...or *was*. Always cheerful and full of life, they are...and for such an advanced age, at that. I'm sure they'll be *absolutely* devastated when they hear about Eudora."

"I don't understand. What do you mean by that? Don't they live across the street from each other?""

"Oh. The Carters are on holiday. They are in Egypt right now and probably don't even know about Eudora."

"I see," the inspector answered.

"Oh, yes. The Carters travel abroad quite often. And they *always* bring a little knickknack back for me. Dust collectors, really. Can you believe it? But it's so sweet of them to think of me. We never had customers who were so thoughtful toward us here in the bank. It must be Miss Carter who is such a good baker I assume. They bring us the most delicious cookies and cakes throughout the year. Oh...and her scrumptious nut bread is to die for!"

16

Arriving at the Luxor train station shortly after dawn, Baako and the three Americans, along with their luggage, were then transported for several miles via motor coach to a dock along the banks of the Nile. They were still tired and groggy from the bumpy, noisy ride from Cairo, but their eyes widened when they saw where they would be spending the next few nights and days. Baako smiled. He had anticipated their reactions.

"A little somewhat more *recent* history there, my friends," he said as he pointed to the side-wheel paddle steamer. "But history nonetheless."

They were about to board the SS Sudan, a steamer that had been built for the Egyptian royal family in 1885. In 1921 it had been transformed into a cruise liner for tourists and had been owned by Thomas Cook & Son until 1950, when it was then purchased by Fouad Pasha Serageddin, and Egyptian politician and leader of the Wafd Party.

"Marcus," Baako said to the still wide-eyed author, "you will not be the first famous author to ride the waters in that steamer. Agatha Christie and her husband cruised the Nile on the Sudan back in 1933 and I have no doubt that the plot for her famous book may have been hatched on her decks."

"Wow," Marcus replied as they walked toward the gangplank, "Baako, You're just *full* of revelations, aren't you?"

But the most startling revelation was yet to come.

The beautiful old steam ship consisted of eighteen cabins and six suites spread across three levels. Marcus and Valencia had been booked into the

Agatha Christie Suite on the upper deck, with Sebastian and Baako being booked into their own separate cabins.

Valencia, especially, was thrilled when they were ushered into their suite, offering panoramic views of the Nile from its broad bay windows. The room was so inviting and relaxing, with dark wood paneling and warm colors of the fabrics and furniture.

"I think I could stay here forever, Marcus," she practically swooned.

And Marcus Darke agreed.

Two hours later, the magnificent old vessel slowly began its journey.

Over the next few days they would cruise to the various tombs and temples along this stretch of the river.

By night, they would dine in high fashion within the plush dining room, with fine linens and crystal glassware. To the Americans' delight, cocktails were available, as the ship was a tourist attraction and alcohol service was permitted.

The Captain of the ship greeted Baako Mustafa, well known by so many, as they sat at the dining table the first night aboard. The Captain was accompanied, at his side, by a wine steward who, with a flourish, presented the guests with a bottle of Dom Pérignon 1952, and then removed the cork with a loud pop, making heads turn from the other diners.

"Baakoo Mustafa," said the Captain with a slight bow, "it is an honor to have you amongst our presence once again. And you three," he said to the Americans, "I am sure by now that you have learned that his knowledge is unlimited. He is wise beyond his years. You shall return to your homes enlightened and quite changed. That I can guarantee."

Baako blushed.

The steward poured the champagne, bowed slightly and left the table. The Captain followed suit.

Yes, the three Americans would be changed in ways they never would have expected.

Perhaps it was the champagne. Or perhaps it was the romantic, brilliant full moon overhead, casting its light on the gently rippling river below. A thousand twinkling diamonds were scattered across the black sky. Marcus and Valencia lay, naked, entwined in each other's arms following the long, slow ecstasy of their lovemaking. Quite different from their love making on the noisy train the night before. They gazed out of the large bay windows at the foot of their bed and saw the silhouettes of massive trees swaying in a soft breeze. Possibly the same scene viewed by Cleopatra and Julius Caesar as they cruised the Nile together on her barge two thousand years earlier. Below the trees, on the ground in darkness, they thought they saw white shapes shining in the moonlight. Something grazing. Perhaps they were camels. Perhaps they were goats. Or perhaps it was the champagne.

The next couple of days, with the cruise first starting out at Dendera Temple, upstream from their starting point, the ship then moved further downstream to the Valley of the Kings, sitting on the west bank of the Nile. This was the principal burial place for the New Kingdom's major royal figures, containing sixty-five tombs and chambers excavated by Egyptologists and archeologists from several countries. The Valley is hidden from sight behind tall cliffs. The three Americans would certainly get an energetic workout here. They were not alone. A few dozen other tourists, some who were aboard the Sudan, wandered from tomb to tomb, some with other guides, some with guide books in hand.

"It is unfortunate," Baako told his trio, "that almost all of the tombs have been opened and robbed long ago but, of course, they will still give you the idea of the opulence and power of our pharaohs."

Baako took them to the various tombs of pharaohs long dead, including the tomb of Tutankhamun. Each elaborate tomb had them walking down steep stairways, deep into the hot sandy ground that was above. The temperature was rising. Some of it became quite strenuous. Marcus' mind was overwhelmed; Valencia's camera was working overtime; and Reckless was getting restless.

But at their next stop, Karnak Temple, a simple question would bring the biggest astonishment of all. One that would shatter some of their long-held beliefs.

17

Karnak Temple, Luxor, Egypt

Karnak Temple is a vast open-air museum and the largest ancient religious site in the world. It is probably the second most visited historical site in Egypt, second only to the Great Pyramids in Giza.

As they walked amongst the towering columns Marcus Darke stopped and looked deep in thought.

"What is it, Marcus?" asked Baako. "You look puzzled."

"I was thinking about something that appears to be missing...or rather, *someone* who appears to be missing in all the things we've observed. We have spent hours in the museum in Cairo and we've seen countless papyri, statues of pharaohs, tomb paintings, etc. so far on this cruise. Of course, *you* seem to be a walking encyclopedia. I know that the Egyptians were exceptional historians. And still are, for that matter. You guys, through the centuries, have written about everything and everybody. Except one guy. I haven't seen any reference *anywhere* to Moses."

Baako Mustafa took a deep breath. His heart started to beat just a bit faster. It wasn't that he feared this question. On very rare occasion he had been asked it before. He simply did not want to offend the people who were paying his fee by his response. His *honest* response.

Marcus, Valencia, and Sebastian stood staring at Baako. Waiting for a reply. A startling reply that would shatter some of their long-held beliefs.

Baako had no idea what reaction he might get from the trio. But the question had been asked and it was his obligation to answer, no matter what the repercussions might be.

"I shall answer that question honestly, Marcus, but I must caution you beforehand. I sincerely hope that it does not offend. We have not discussed *your* religion at all so far on this trip, only *ours*, here in Egypt."

"And?"

Baako took another deep breath.

"Moses is a very important character in *your* religion. In *your* Bible. But Moses has no place in *our* history."

"Wait a minute," Valencia said with a look of confusion on her face. "By saying that he has no place in your *history*, does that mean that the early Egyptians didn't write about him…or are you saying that he simply did not exist?"

A brief pause. A brief silence.

"I'm saying that he did not really exist," Baako finally replied succinctly.

The three Americans stood back in disbelief.

"Okay," Sebastian Reckling said, looking even more confused than Valencia, "you mean there was no little baby in a basket floating down the Nile? No bulrushes?"

"Yes," answered Baako, "that's what I'm saying."

"But then…what about the plagues…'Pharaoh, let my people go'…the exodus…all that stuff? Oh, and what, then, about the Ten Commandments. You know…all that *thou shalt not* stuff?"

Baako actually had to laugh at that very last part.

"Look, your Bible was written by dozens of men, over countless decades. Some of them had very good imaginations. They also must have done some extensive research. Research into *our* history. Egyptian history. The Ten Commandments? *Long* before your Bible was written we had the Forty-two Negative Confessions. These would lead our recently deceased into their afterlife. It is more of a *I have not* sort of thing as opposed to a *thou shalt not* sort of thing. I already told you about the Book of the Dead. We already discussed that at the Cairo Museum. Whoever wrote the parts in the Bible regarding the Ten Commandments evidently handpicked ten of our Negative Confessions. And there they are. Almost word for word."

"So, let me get this straight," said a very confused and concerned Marcus Darke, "what you are implying is that Moses…you called him a *character*, as in *fictional* character…simply did not exist."

"I'm not *implying* it. I'm stating it," answered Baako Mustafa. "Moses is far more myth than fact. Myth and metaphor."

Baako suddenly stopped talking and motioned for them all to follow him down an adjoining colonnade. A large tour group was heading their way and he didn't want them to overhear what they were discussing.

The guide leading that group recognized Baako, calling out to him and waving. Baako smiled, nodded and waved back.

The three Americans were dumbfounded. This was *not* the lecture they were expecting at all.

"Baako," said Marcus with a concerned look on his face once again, "regarding our Bible, have you even *read*..."

"Of course, I've read it, Marcus. It is filled with fact and fiction. Myth and metaphor, as I just said. History and histrionics. As *all* religions are. I have studied many religions beyond my own. But there *is* a limit to my research and knowledge. It is theorized that there are over four thousand religions of all types in our wide world right now. You know what that leads to? There are at least eighteen thousand gods, goddesses and animals of all types being worshipped. Astonishing, isn't it? In several religions there are stories regarding death and resurrection...including our own revered Isis and Osiris...that predate the story of Jesus and *his* death and resurrection."

"Thank God I'm an atheist," Sebastian joked sarcastically. Valencia simply rolled her eyes.

But, as hard as he tried, Sebastian Reckling could not detect a single lie in what the young Egyptian was saying.

The three Americans stood in stunned silence, again, exchanging glances.

Marcus Darke stood with his hands on his hips, shaking his head.

"Hot damn and holy shit, young man. Baako, I'm *certainly* getting my money's worth with *you* for our guide. Jesus Christ...no pun intended there...but here I thought we'd be learning just about all these fucking tombs and temples."

Baako Mustafa laughed, relieved now that the reaction from the trio hadn't been catastrophic. But he was still a bit apprehensive.

"I hope to see some of what you have learned from me in your next publication, Marcus Darke. Just as long as you don't write about a fictional tour guide and kill him off because of what I just said. Or worse...have *him* be the killer!"

After taking a few moments to absorb what Baako had just told them, the group finally started to meander once again through the temple.

"I may or may not fully understand or even agree with what you just said, but what amazes me the *most*, Baako," Valencia Darke finally spoke up, "aside from your incredible knowledge is your superb command of the English language. Aside from your delightful accent, you speak much better than most of the friends we have back in New York City!"

Baako chuckled, making a slight bow with bit of a flourish.

"Very similar to our beloved ancient Queen Cleopatra, Valencia, it appears that you are fluent in flattery."

With her mind still reeling from what Baako had just said about Moses, Valencia slowly wandered away from her group to take more photographs of the massive structure. She wanted pictures without other tourists in them. She pointed her camera upwards, focusing on the brilliantly painted ceiling with intricate, colorful artwork. Her camera's telephoto lens captured the ancient artwork, her shutter clicking away furiously. She was mesmerized and deep in thought as she turned down another colonnade devoid of people.

She looked down just in time to see the cobra.

The deadly Egyptian cobra can grow to be quite large, possibly up to four and a half feet in length. This one was large. And only a few feet away.

The snake was as surprised to see Valencia as she was to see the snake. The snake suddenly rose up into striking position, spreading its hood, fixing Valencia with its gaze. She immediately thought of the hooded cobra on the front of Tutankhamun's golden Death Mask at the Cairo Museum. Valencia knew that this was not good.

A moment later, the three men heard Valencia scream and instantly rushed around the corner of the colonnade.

She was lying, motionless, on the ground at the base of one of the massive columns.

18

Valencia, mustering all the bravery that she could, had carefully, slowly…perhaps foolishly… removed her big, floppy yellow hat and tossed it at the cobra. She was hoping to distract it allowing her to escape. The cobra violently struck out at the hat and, as it did so, Valencia had let out that piercing scream. She then felt faint and slowly slid down the side of the column until she hit the ground.

Marcus panicked when he saw his wife lying on the ground, his heart rate immediately racing as he rushed to her side.

"Val!" he screamed in fear, "Valencia…Jesus Christ…what the fuck is going on?"

She slowly opened her eyes and suddenly jolted back, looking for the snake.

Baako and Sebastian bent down by her side as well. Baako was concerned about the situation and his heart was racing as well.

"Were you just attacked by someone?" he asked cautiously, looking all around. There were always several beggars in galabiyas roaming throughout the historic sites hoping for a few coins from tourists. They might be a nuisance, but they were never aggressive or threatening in any way. He was not aware of tourists ever being attacked by anyone, but there was always a first time. Especially at this time, when Egyptian tempers were on edge and swiftly rising.

Valencia pointed at her hat several feet away from them.

"Is it still there?" she asked. "Be careful!"

"Your hat?" Marcus asked, confused. "Yes, it's there. Why?"

Valencia slowly sat up, and then tried to stand. She was still a bit wobbly but stood with Marcus' help.

"A snake," she said. "A *big* snake! It was a cobra…right there!"

She explained what happened. Baako was relieved that she had not been attacked by a person, but concerned that the cobra, plentiful in Egypt but nocturnal as rule, was slithering among the ruins in broad daylight. A very rare occurrence.

For some reason, at that moment Baako remembered what his friend, Hossam Mahfouz, had said the day before the Americans were to arrive in Egypt. Baako had told his friend that the author intended to write a murder mystery based in Egypt.

"God's willing," Hossam had said, "They won't stir up any of our Djinn, my young friend. I fear that in these troubling times they would be too eager to take vengeance on rabble-rousers, Egyptian or otherwise. Written or otherwise."

Baako Mustafa certainly did not believe in such things as the Djinn. Legend has it that the Djinn can manifest themselves as animals…even snakes, for that matter. He was not superstitious at all, but was the sudden surprising appearance of the cobra foretelling something more ominous?

The group moved on to the nearby Luxor Temple, but both Valencia and Baako kept their eyes peeled for more potential danger.

19

Cairo, Egypt - January 26, 1952 – Black Saturday

What had been a clear blue sky soon blackened as the smoke from the first fire soon spread from building to building. The conflagration was now out of control. Voices raised in anger intermingled with those in panic as the mobs spread through the streets like rushing water through a just-opened sluice.

The Battle of Ismailia, an attack on an Egyptian police installation by British forces the day before, was a direct trigger of the riots. Over fifty auxiliary policemen were killed. The word spread as rapidly as the devastating fires that followed to Cairo. Anti-British protests followed these deaths and were seized upon by organized factions in the crowd. With the unexplained absence of security forces, the angry mobs burned and ransacked large sections of Cairo. Although the attacks seemed to be aimed at British and western-held establishments, the resultant fires were indiscriminate. The perpetrators of the chaos remain unknown to this day, and the truth…the *actual* truth…about this event has yet to be established. Many thought, however, that these devastating riots might have signaled the end of the Kingdom of Egypt. They were correct.

The resultant political and domestic instability paved the way for the Egyptian Revolution of 1952 six months later. A coup resulted in the forced abdication of the king, Farouk I, and the abolition of the monarchy one year later. Further hostilities with the British ensued, but the last British troops stationed in Egypt left the country in June of 1956.

Marcus, Valencia, and Sebastian were standing together on the upper deck of the ship watching the landscape slowly drift by. The wide expanse of land was lush green grasses on either side of the river and with soft rolling peaks of mountains in the distance to the west. Thick stands of various types of trees ran for miles in both directions behind the grasses. Valencia was snapping photo after photo, and Marcus was scribbling notes, describing the hills to the west. Words that would be used in his next book. He was trying to capture the moment. The scene was serene and beautiful. A felucca sailed lazily alongside the steamer and its young sailor waved up to the trio on the deck. And they all waved back.

Sebastian was sipping a short glass of Bourbon on the rocks, and Valencia was sipping some white wine. The air smelled crisp and clean.

Marcus Darke looked up from his notebook when he noticed Baako approaching across the deck.

"Well, finally!" he said with a chuckle. "You were missing for so long we thought that you had fallen over…"

He stopped abruptly when he saw the look on Baako's face. A look of concern, combined with that of anger.

"My worst fears have come to pass," the Egyptian said. "Cairo is in chaos at this very minute. The Captain and I were just on the boat's radio communication system. The situation is getting progressively worse."

Baako Mustafa explained to the trio what was transpiring as best as he knew. He only knew, now, that his three travelers, being westerners, might be in danger. Rage against the British occupation had reached beyond the boiling point. Angry, rampaging mobs won't stop to ask Caucasian tourists if they are British, French, American or other.

"I have no idea what will happen at this point," Baako continued. "But I must get you out of our country safely. And fast. Martial law has just been declared in Cairo and there is a curfew in place. No one allowed on the streets from 9 P.M until 6 A.M."

They all stood in stunned silence for a moment.

"I know a local clothing shop in a small town nearby," Baako finally said. "We shall get off the boat and buy galabiyas for all of you. Turbans for you two men and a head scarf for you, Valencia. You must cover up your blonde hair. Just in case."

"But…" Sebastian Reckling began.

Baako interrupted.

"Our boat will now be heading back to Luxor. The man owning this vessel has ordered his ship to return to the safety of its homeport. We must not continue on, I'm sorry to say. Abu Simbel, as remote as it is, is no longer on our itinerary out of fear of what might be happening. I was on the radio system also with the Mena House in Giza. They are safe. The fires and rioters have not reached them. The conflict is raging in the opposite direction. But many of their guests are foolishly fleeing in panic. We will take the train back to Cairo and I have secured rooms again for you there at the hotel."

"But..." Sebastian began once again, only to be interrupted by Baako once again.

"God's willing, we will be able to get from the train station safely once we're back in Cairo and get you to the hotel. From there you must contact your airline for passage out of Egypt."

An exodus.

"But," Sebastian started for the third time, "unless those roving gangs are pirates, wouldn't all the boats...and us...be safer out here in the middle of this wide river than going back to port somewhere?"

Baako nodded, and then shrugged his shoulders.

"I agree, but I cannot argue. We are but passengers on this vessel and the Captain has his orders from his superiors. What's done cannot be undone."

A little more than twenty-four hours later, Baako led the American trio, now *almost* resembling fellow Egyptians clad in native garb, from the train station to an awaiting taxicab. It was one of the rare few vehicles still out and about. The streets appeared to be eerily quiet, with very few pedestrians and nary a police or military officer, but the air was putrid, still lingering with the pungent odors of fire, smoke, and death.

The car had traveled less than two dark, narrow blocks from the train station when a young man ran out from the shadows of an alleyway and stepped directly in front of the car to flag them down. He looked deranged and was brandishing a pistol, pointing it straight at the windshield. The car came to a halt.

Baako Mustafa, who was sitting in the front seat alongside the driver, held his breath.

"This is not good," he whispered in Arabic.

20

The taxicab driver rolled his eyes.

Holding the steering wheel firmly in both hands, the driver yelled "Ahmaq sakhif! *Fucking idiot*," and, without hesitation, stomped his foot down on the gas pedal.

The car plowed straight into the man, sending him flying in one direction and his gun in the other.

Valencia screamed, Marcus closed his eyes, and Sebastian tried not to wet himself.

The car continued speeding away from the scene. Baako, looking into the car's side view mirror to his right, saw that the young man got up on his feet and hobbled off. Injured, yes, but not dead.

"Well played," Baako said to the driver in Arabic. "Not too smart, but well played."

"What the *hell* just happened there?" Marcus asked breathlessly.

"It was just a quick glance, but I have seen that look in young men's faces before. There's no way of knowing for sure," answered Baako, "but just the look in that fellow's eyes told me he may have been on drugs. Hashish, probably. I doubt that it had anything to do with the riots but, as I said, there's no way of knowing that. More than likely he was going to rob us. A brash, stupid thing for him to do. Something else for you to write about, Marcus."

Thirty minutes later the taxi pulled into the portico of the Mena House. The three Americans got stares from the staff as they, dressed in galabiyas, strode into the lobby, Baako right behind them.

But Baako stopped before they had gotten too far. He hadn't expected that their journey would have to come to an end so abruptly.

This was the part that had always made him emotional when leaving his groups of tourists after their time together. Sometimes he was glad to see them go, a few of them, anyway. Sometimes he felt a little melancholy. But this little trio had been different. They were quite special. They had bonded in a unique way.

Baako took a deep breath as the three Americans stared at him in silence.

"I shall have to say my goodbyes here, then," the Egyptian said abruptly. He was visibly shaken. "I regret that our time here has been cut short by circumstances but surely, Marcus, I hope that you have accomplished your goals with enough material for your book."

The three Americans stood with sadness apparent on their faces.

"Oh, I have, my friend, indeed I have," Marcus replied with a broad smile.

"Far more than I could have hoped for. But I understand your position."

Baako sighed deeply.

"Please. You need pay me no more than what you have already with your deposit, Marcus. I have thoroughly enjoyed our time together. These past days have been special. You three are far more than tourists to me now. It's been fun...up to a point, of course. But I cannot..."

"Oh, no, no, Baako," Marcus interrupted shaking his head. "That's not right. I shall not accept that. This trip was the *best*. The three of us... speaking for the other two...have been overwhelmed. And you are now far more than a guide to us. I shall reward you with payment in full as agreed upon weeks ago. You have gone to great expense, thought, and time to put this journey together. No argument from you, you hear?"

Baako reluctantly nodded.

Sebastian Reckling turned to Baako with tears in his eyes. An emotion Sebastian rarely felt.

"Mr. Mustafa," he said, shaking Baako's hand so firmly that the Egyptian almost winced, "you are truly an amazing young man. As that Captain on the Sudan said, you are wise beyond your years. Thank you for what you have done for *me*, Marcus aside."

Valencia was now in tears herself.

"Baako," she said sniffling softly. "I knew this time would have to come, but I'm not prepared for it now. You have no idea how I shall miss you. I shall never, *ever* forget you and this adventure. Thank you for being who you are. If and when you may ever decide to have a wife and children, they will be getting the best husband and father possible."

She leaned in, giving him a firm hug that went on seemingly for minutes. She then reached up kissing him on the cheek.

Marcus took Baako by the shoulders and looked him squarely in the eyes.

"I will never be able to thank you enough. These past days have been exceptional. This will be my best book ever thanks to you, my friend. I have no doubt. Perhaps we shall meet again. Come see us in New York."

"Tirooh was tigi bis salaama!" Baako said, voice cracking, as he swiftly turned to leave. "Have a safe trip!"

And with that, Baako Mustafa was a silhouette as he walked out into the bright rising sun of a new day.

Not only would Marcus Darke wire the full agreed upon fee into Baako's account when he got back home, he would add a bonus of two thousand dollars.

21

Marcus, Valencia and Sebastian would then have to wait at the hotel for at least forty-eight hours before they could get a flight back into the United States from Cairo. Fearful fleeing tourists had booked every available flight, no matter the destinations. They simply wanted to flee from danger.

Marcus Darke took full advantage of this situation, not wasting any time. He and Sebastian sat, side-by-side, out on the poolside terrace of the Mena House while he scribbled away in his notebook, with a story outline already forming. He and Sebastian, together, were developing characters, motivations, and potential outcomes.

But Marcus had noticed something different in his friend's attitude.

"Reckless," he said, looking up from his notebook for a moment. "You seem more pensive than I've seen you in ages. Well,...in *forever*, for that matter. What's up?"

Sebastian Reckling was watching a flock of birds swoop around the top of the pyramid. The one from which he nearly died. He sighed and shook his head.

"This trip," he replied wistfully, "turned out to be far more than I was prepared for. Certainly different, that's for damn sure. I am sincerely grateful for your invitation and for this opportunity. Who knew, right?"

"Who knew *what*, Reckless?"

No answer came.

Marcus watched as Valencia swam lazily back and forth in the warm pool. And Sebastian was on his third Gin Rickey.

Manal Khalifa saw them sitting out on the terrace and came to sit with them. Most of the hotel guests had departed; many of them in panicked haste, and no tours were being planned. It would probably take quite a while for Egyptian tourism to regain its strength. But it would return.

Valencia had stepped from the pool and was wrapping a towel around her as the young woman approached.

"Any word, yet, about your brother, Manal?" she asked.

Manal looked forlorn.

"No, not yet," she sighed. "Inspector Mohammadi has called a few times, still asking questions after questions. No word, and no clues. I wonder if my brother will *ever* be found. With all the riots a few days ago he may be lost forever."

"Don't give up hope, Manal." Marcus chimed in.

Manal feared the worst. And she would be correct.

Finally, later that afternoon, the trio got word that a flight had opened departing Cairo later that evening for Paris. Tickets in First Class were available and Marcus booked them immediately. A two-hour layover in Paris. They would then connect with a flight to Boston, before then heading to Idlewild in New York City. Long, tiring, but none of that mattered to the trio.

They were going home.

The corridors of the airport were crowded and noisy.

"For the love of Pete," Marcus Darke exclaimed as he saw two familiar faces coming toward them. The Carter twins.

"What a surprise," Marcus said as he stopped to say hello.

Needless to say, the twins were just as surprised to see the Americans approaching.

"I guess both of our trips have been cut short, haven't they," Adam Carter said, as Adeline stood back and glowered at Sebastian Reckling. "Did you get what you hoped for?" Adam asked Marcus.

"Yes, yes," Marcus answered. "Unfortunately we couldn't get everywhere I had hoped, but it was still an adventure I can classify as successful. How about you two?"

"Oh," chuckled Adeline, "we got *much* more than we had hoped."

The Carter twins exchanged a secret smile.

The Carters had reached their departure gate just as the final call for boarding was being given. Adam hurried ahead.

Adeline stopped.

She stared Marcus right in the eye.

"Just for future reference, Mr. Mystery Writer," Adeline said with a chuckle, wattle wagging beneath her chin, "there *is* such a thing as a perfect murder. Perhaps several of them. Trust me...I know."

She quickly turned on her heels and followed her brother, disappearing into the ramp leading to their awaiting airplane.

"What the hell was *that* supposed to mean?" Marcus said with a frown.

Sebastian shook his head slowly.

"I told you, Marcus, a couple weeks ago when we were with them for a while. Something about those two old goats seemed...well, off. And I shall tell you again now, they are not who they appear to be. They are both very proficient liars. Obviously. Perhaps even more than that. I repeat what *she* just said; trust me, I know."

"But," Valencia chimed in, "what's the big deal now? They're gone. Off to somewhere in the boondocks of England. And soon *we'll* be back in the States. What's to come from your observations, Reckless? And why even bother?"

"Val's right," Marcus Darke said. "Why bother? And who cares? For Christ's sake, Reckless, everybody lies. We *all* lie. Doesn't mean that we're bad people. Come on...our flight's boarding."

Sebastian Reckling shrugged his shoulders and remained silent.

PART THREE

Final Destinations

One will inevitably meet one's destiny.
Egyptian Proverb

22

There was the familiar bump as the airplane's wheels touched down onto the runway, followed by a smattering of applause from grateful passengers.

"Welcome to New York's Idlewild Airport, ladies and gentlemen," said the soothing voice of a stewardess over the intercom, "your final destination on flight eight-twenty-two from Boston. Please remain in your seats with your seatbelts fastened until the Captain guides our plane to the assigned gate at the terminal."

Marcus Darke let out a little chuckle.

"Don't you love their fatalistic terminology?" he said, leaning into Valencia who was slowly awakening. "I mean, really...*final destination* sounds like we've arrived at death and will be greeted by the Grim Reaper, who then leads us into Purgatory. And *terminal* really puts that final nail in the coffin."

Valencia yawned and stretched.

"I'll just bet you think you're the only person who has ever said that," she said, stifling another yawn. "Not very original...Mr. Mystery Writer." And she laughed.

Marcus turned around behind them to see if Sebastian was awake, but he wasn't in his seat.

"Where the hell did Reckless go?" he asked Valencia. She shrugged her shoulders and yawned once again.

The airplane was slowly rolling toward the gate when Sebastian walked up the aisle and quickly took his seat. Marcus noticed his return and leaned over his seat back to talk to him.

"Want to share our cab back into town or are you getting back up to Scarsdale from here?"

"Well, actually," Sebastian answered rather sheepishly, "there's this stewardess back there in the steerage section, and…"

"Jesus Christ, Reckless!" Marcus cut him off. "That's *so* cliché. A stewardess? Really? Spare us the details if you're now a member of the Mile High Club. Grow up."

"Now wait just a damn minute," Sebastian said, a bit on the defensive side. "It's not what you're thinking at all. I *know* that stewardess. We used to date not too long ago. We became very close. She broke it off when she found out that I was married. Well, I *was* at that time. We just had a long talk. A very *long*, honest to god talk. I like her. I mean, I *really* like her. I've changed. And she's the same beautiful lady. And by the way, I live in New Rochelle…not Scarsdale, asshole."

Cairo, Egypt

Almost at that exact moment, Baako Mustafa was once again walking down the winding corridors of Khan el-Kalili Bazaar when he saw his old friend Hossam Mahfouz sitting at his favorite spot at the coffeehouse. Baako had been extremely concerned about his friend and worried about the old man's safety during the riots. The old man jumped up from his seat.

The two men embraced, each had been worried about the other.

"Ah, Baako," the old man said with outstretched arms and wide eyes. "So glad to see you again, my young friend. I warned you, didn't I? I just *knew* something bad would happen. And now we are both safe. The Djinn have retreated."

"For now, anyway," Baako said. "But I'm sure it's not over. There will be more trouble ahead for Egypt. We must remain vigilant."

"But, good news!" Hossam exclaimed loudly, almost jumping up and down. "Good news! I protected that special widow from some of the rioters as they raced, yelling and screaming, past her house and now she has finally agreed to marry me! She say I was very brave. Can you believe that? Yes, we shall marry. Even if I smell like horse. Now *she* will smell like horse!"

Baako laughed until tears were streaming down his face.

Yes, Hossam's life had been delightfully changed in the most unexpected way.

It was Inspector Ahmed Mohammadi's obligation to tell the Kahlifa family about the death of Aharon, Manal's brother. But it was ugly. And had been brutal. Telling them wouldn't be easy. Should he leave out the horrible details?

The day after the riots, as Cairo was slowly recovering from the intense devastation, the Inspector had been called to a partially burned out building in Manshiyat Nassar, appropriately nicknamed Garbage City. It was a slum city just around the corner from Cairo's center, at the base of Mokattam Hill.

When he had approached the building, a police officer that was among the group cordoning off the area came forward to warn him. The officer shook his head.

Inspector Mohammadi slowly climbed the garbage-strewn stairs up to the top floor, the seventh. Several other officers were in front of one of the open doors. Obviously the scene of the crime. The inspector couldn't tell if he was smelling garbage or death at this point. The men stepped aside as he entered the room.

The decomposing body of a young man lay spread-eagled tied to the bedposts. Mohammadi came closer and bent down, examining the body. There were little burn marks all over parts of the body, probably made from the ends of lit cigarettes. On his chest, face, arms, and legs. This man had been slowly tortured before death. It got worse.

There were burn marks on the dead man's scrotum…but it was even worse than that.

The man's penis had been severed and was stuffed into his mouth.

The medical examiner would determine that, aside from losing a lot of blood, the man had choked and suffocated to death on his own manhood.

How could he tell the man's parents?

But first he had to inform the dead man's wife.

"How can you be sure it's Aharon?" Esa, his wife asked, almost defiantly.

Two little faces were peeking around the corner of the living room as Mohammadi spoke.

"Go!" the mother shouted to her children. "Go back to the kitchen with your uncle. Go!"

They scampered away.

"I repeat," the distraught woman said again, "how do you know it was my husband? You said he was unclothed. You had no photograph of the man, did you?"

The Inspector waited a beat before answering.

"Whoever it was that did this to your husband, Mrs. Kahlifa, just threw his clothing all around the room. There must have been quite a struggle, because his clothes were ripped from his body and covered in blood. His attacker...or attackers didn't bother to conceal them in any way. His driver's license was in his pocket."

Another man appeared in the room, coming from the back of the house. He was dark and brooding. Not a friendly looking face at all.

"This is my brother," the newly widowed woman said, looking up. "Sobeck, this is Inspector Mohammadi," she said, introducing the two men. "As I have feared, Aharon is dead. He was murdered."

Sobeck Salim remained expressionless, lighting up a cigarette. Something caught the Inspector's attention. The knuckles on Sobeck's right hand appeared to be rough and bruised.

"Who has taken this man from my sister?" Sobeck asked after a moment of silent staring.

"I'm sorry to say," Inspector Mohammadi responded, "at this point we do not know. Perhaps we shall *never* know. The riots a few days ago may be a part of it. But...somehow I doubt it."

Interesting name, Sobeck Inspector Mohammadi thought to himself. *Rarely is that name used these days I would imagine.*

Sobeck was one of the oldest of the ancient Egyptian deities. He is often depicted as a crocodile-headed human. He could be a protective deity, protecting the innocent...but also could be aggressive and violent.

Inspector Mohammadi took note of the fact that neither the widow nor her brother seemed to show any remorse about what was just divulged.

23

Swaffham, England

Detective Chief Inspector Weldon Atherstone had earned the nickname "Well-Done" from all his fellow officers at the precinct because of his tenacious methods of solving crimes. And he *always* solved them. Burglaries and robberies had been the main crimes locally, with relatively few murders. There were perhaps only seven or eight hundred murders per year in the whole of the United Kingdom, most of them not mysteries at all. A fight in a pub. Domestic arguments that got out of hand. Gang fights, etc. His town was basically a quiet, crime-free town as a rule.

Atherstone sat back into his chair at his desk; perplexed by the very long telephone call he had just ended. A surprising telephone call out of the blue with unexpected results. At first he didn't believe what he had just been told…but then, why would the man lie? For what purpose? He was almost assured of his conclusion regarding the death of Eudora Smythe, but he needed to make absolutely sure. This telephone call made one thing perfectly clear. He needed to meet the Carters. He also needed to be cautious. Very cautious.

It was late afternoon on that gloomy day. His car rolled to a stop in front of the Carter's house and he stepped out. There was chilling mist beginning to fall. The air was even colder and he pulled his collar up around his neck. The Inspector glanced up at the house, which was well over a hundred years old, surrounded by tall trees that were even older. He turned around and took a short glance at the smaller house across the street. Now dark and empty. Eudora Smythe's house. The scene of a crime.

He shook his head, sighed and walked up the front steps onto the broad front porch.

Adeline Carter had just put the kettle on for some tea when the doorbell rang.

"I shall get it, dear," said Adam.

He walked through the small foyer and opened the front door to face a man he'd never seen before.

"Good afternoon, Mr. Carter," said the man. "I'm Detective Chief Inspector Weldon Atherstone. I'm sorry to intrude, but might I have a word with you and your sister?"

"Oh, my goodness gracious me, sir, but of course. Come on in...I see that it's just now beginning to rain. You mustn't get wet, now, should you?"

Adam, with a tinge of nervousness about this unexpected visit, ushered the inspector in and took his coat, hanging it on a rack by the front door. The Inspector followed Adam, glancing around as they entered the large, over-stuffed living room. The color scheme tended towards the dark. Burgundy sofa, hunter green side chair, deep mahogany paneling. Persian carpets on the dark hardwood floors. Everything looked old. It smelled old. There were knickknacks everywhere. On shelves, on little tables, especially along the mantle over the fireplace. He saw a miniature Eiffel Tower, a small sphinx, something that looked like the Empire State Building, and another cheap rendition of Big Ben. He noticed things like that.

"Please, have a seat...oh, here's Adeline now," he said as his sibling slowly entered the room.

"Good afternoon, Miss Carter," said the inspector, tipping his head slightly, introducing himself to her, and then sitting on a big high-backed upholstered chair that had seen better days. "If you don't mind, I just want to ask a few questions about your neighbor, Eudora Smythe."

"Oh, my goodness," exclaimed Adeline. If she had been wearing pearls she would be clutching them. "Poor, poor Eudora. A tragedy, to be sure. I was shocked when I heard about the poor sweet woman's death. *Shocked*, I tell you! Of course, we were on holiday in Egypt when it happened and..."

"Actually," interrupted Atherstone inhaling deeply and watching Adeline's reaction, "she died before you even left England. That's why I need to discuss something with you. Something that troubles me greatly. She left a puzzling clue. I've spoken to a few other people who were familiar with her. And familiar with the both of *you*. I've gotten some conflicting and puzzling responses. Frankly left me scratching my head for a while. And just a few hours ago I learned something completely new. Therefore I have arrived at a surprising and unsettling deduction. You're not *really* related to Howard Carter, are you?"

He stared silently at the both of them, waiting for a reaction.

Adeline and Adam looked at one another. *Trapped!*

The Inspector quickly and deliberately changed the subject. He wanted to catch them off guard.

"Did you both enjoy your holiday?"

That question momentarily threw them both for a loop.

"Actually, we did," Adeline answered, a bit befuddled. "Aside from that little nastiness in Cairo. You probably read about *that*. Apparently they hate us Brits. Fortunately that did not affect us. We just had to cut our time short. Very enlightening, though. We brought home some *wonderful* souvenirs. I even brought back a little gift to give to our good friend Eudora. I always did that when we travel. She loves…well, *loved* her sweet little old pussycat so I brought her a little alabaster statuette of Bastet, an Egyptian cat goddess."

The sound of the teakettle whistling interrupted the conversation.

"Oh," Adeline said abruptly, "we were just about to have a spot of tea. Actually it's Egyptian tea…hibiscus. They call it karkade. We brought some of it back with us. They serve it chilled down there but it's wonderful hot as well. A perfect day for some. May I get you a cup?"

"No, thank you, Miss Carter, I…"

"Oh give it a try, Inspector. It is *so* soothing and we're discussing an unpleasant occurrence regarding dear, sweet Eudora."

"Well…alright. Just one cup and I then need to ask a few more unpleasant questions, I'm afraid."

"Do you need any help out there, dear?" Adam asked.

"Oh, no, dear, I'll handle it just fine. You know me," and she chuckled, winking at her brother.

The two men sat in silence, exchanging slight, polite smiles as they waited.

This is not going to end well, Adam thought to himself.

This is not going to be easy, Artherstone thought to himself.

Adeline took matters into her own hands. Yes, she did. Just that.

Two minutes later Adeline carried two cups of tea into the room, handing one to Adam first, and then to the Inspector. She and Adam exchanged winks.

"Oh, my," the inspector said, "what an unusual color. Crimson red. It's beautiful."

She went back into the kitchen to get her own cup of tea, returning quickly.

"It tastes as good as it looks, Inspector," Adeline said as she watched him raise the cup to his lips.

But he didn't take a sip. He had merely taken a whiff of its aroma. He lowered the cup once again. He could tell the temperature of the tea was too hot for him. He preferred it tepid.

"Now, then," Atherstone began, "as I said, I have a few conflicting statements from other people regarding your relationship with Miss Smythe. I must say that I'm a bit confused. You say that she was a dear friend but…"

He cocked his head, with a quizzical look on his face, and paused.

Adam Carter had sipped from his cup and had gotten a peculiar look on *his* face, making an unusual sound.

"Addy!…What did you…" Adam Carter said as he glared at his sister. He dropped his cup, spilling what little tea was left down the front of his shirt and slumped back into the chair.

"A perfect pot of tea takes time to brew properly, doesn't it, Inspector Atherstone?" Adeline said with a smile.

The inspector was confused.

"It's been fun, hasn't it, dear, all these years?" Adeline said as she looked at her brother, now slumped motionless in his chair. There were tears in her eyes.

Suddenly Inspector Atherstone grasped what was happening. He quickly put down his cup on the small table that was by his chair and leaped to his feet.

"We came into this world together, Addy, and we're leaving it together," the old woman said.

Adeline Carter was on the opposite side of the room, but the inspector lunged for her anyway.

"No!" he screamed.

But it was too late. Adeline Carter swallowed the entire cup of the tea in one gulp and collapsed in a heap. She was probably dead before she even hit the floor.

Hemlock, wolfsbane, and opium. Cleopatra's favorite poison. Painless and swift.

Adeline and Adam had vowed years ago, that should a time such as this ever come, if at all possible they would never be taken alive for their crimes.

Momentarily stunned by what he had just witnessed, Weldon Atherstone was so positive that one or both of the Carter twins had murdered Eudora Smythe that he had two constables waiting in their car out in front of the house. He had to step over Adeline's body to get to the front door to motion for them to come in. No longer to make an arrest, but to observe and be told what had just happened.

Still totally perplexed by that long-distance telephone call earlier in the afternoon, he stood waiting for the medical examiner to arrive. He thought about the man who had called him, after taking the time and effort of tracking him down somehow over the telephone service, all the way from New York City. The inspector had never, ever heard of a Forensic Linguistic Specialist.

Must be something quite new in the States, he thought to himself.

Although he had had no intention of drinking the tea Adeline had given to him, he later found out that it had *not* been laced with poison.

What followed, then, was a complicated mess of legal entanglements. The Carters had no surviving relatives to inherit their respective estates under the rules of intestacy, therefore their estates passed to the Crown. This is known as bona vacantia. The Treasury Solicitor is responsible for dealing with the estate at that point. As it turned out, the Carter twins were multimillionaires, including their stocks, bank accounts, real estate and thousands of pieces of jewelry, men's and women's, found in dozens of drawers, boxes, and trunks throughout the house.

Among the hundreds of pieces of jewelry was a thin gold chain with a strange amulet. The eye of Horus. Back in Egypt, Manal Kahlifa had been distraught when she discovered that it was missing. She couldn't fathom how or when she had lost it. But then Baako Mustafa bought her a new one.

Most alarming and damning to the authorities in Swaffham was the discovery of vials of various deadly poisons in the Carter house pantry. Dozens of them. The authorities were astounded and questioned how on Earth Adeline could have gotten all the ingredients for such deadly potions.

The Public Health council was legally obligated to organize funerals, albeit no-frills, for both of the twins. Their final destinations determined by the Crown.

The Carter twins may have avoided justice being served in *this* life, but their hearts were definitely *not* lighter than a feather in the afterlife.

Weldon, "Well-Done", Atherstone was roundly congratulated for solving yet another crime, heinous as it had been. But the remaining murders committed by the twins remained unsolved. Perhaps in time they would be, or maybe not. But it would take time. Perfect murders, indeed, for now. And death comes as the end.

Sebastian Reckling's professionally trained instincts and innate abilities were always working. Even while he was on vacation, and much to his own chagrin at times. Those instincts were catalysts that destroyed at least one of his romantic relationships in the recent past.

He had *vaguely* remembered the name of the town where the Carters had said they lived, but he remembered *vividly* that they said it was where their supposed relative, Howard Carter, lived. That fact he could easily research. He was so uncomfortable with his feelings toward the old couple that he eventually was able to contact, via a long-distance telephone call, a police department office and then a detective in Swaffham, England. He had nothing to gain from this endeavor except his own personal and professional satisfaction.

Detective Chief Inspector Weldon Atherstone, at first, was confused by this strange telephone call. He didn't understand what the man was trying to say. Or why. The man in New York City asked him if there had been any strange, unsolved crimes in the town recently…more specifically, a murder.

And that's when the conversation soon got around to the name of Adeline.

And that's when the dots had connected.

24

February 14, 1952
NEW YORK CITY – 5:15 P.M.

Marcus Darke, in his tenth floor apartment at 220 Sutton Place South, stood at his living room widow overlooking the East River. He watched as the traffic moved briskly across the Queensboro Bridge, commuters eager to get home and out of the cold wintry air. The temperature had barely climbed above freezing all day and, fortunately, the snow that had been predicted never arrived.

He was wearing the galabiya that he had purchased in Luxor before their somewhat hasty retreat homeward.

He noticed movement behind him in the window's reflection and he turned to face Valencia who was approaching with two Gin Rickeys in her hands. She, too, was wearing a galabiya.

"Those Egyptians really had something going, didn't they? These things are comfortable," Valencia said.

Marcus smiled, kissed her gently on the lips and took one of the glasses. They toasted a Happy Valentine's Day to each other and took a few sips. They slowly walked over to one of the living room walls where several framed photos were hanging. Valencia's photos.

"Certainly a bit different temperature these days than where we were a few weeks ago," Marcus said as they looked at some of the photos Valencia had taken in Egypt.

Valencia laughed.

Two of the photos, hanging side by side, were of the three men, Marcus,

Sebastian Reckling, and Baako Mustafa prior to and just after their climb up to the top of the Pyramid of Khufu.

Marcus chuckled as he looked at the expression on Sebastian's face in the photo taken just after the climb and they were back down on the sands.

"Reckless certainly changed that day, didn't he?" Valencia snickered.

"We *all* changed that day, Val," Marcus replied. "I think we *all* did."

Valencia slowly placed the tip of her index finger on the image of the smiling handsome young Egyptian, tapping it lightly.

"I miss Baako," Valencia said with a smile.

"So do I, Valencia," Marcus said wistfully. "So do I. I hope he's safe."

"I hope he's happy," Valencia answered.

Giza, Egypt

It was just past dawn as Baako Mustafa galloped his sleek black horse, Khufu, across the Western Desert. The Great Pyramids were not too far in the distance behind him, partially hidden by the morning mists. He turned his head around and smiled as he saw Manal Kahlifa on one of his other horses, Ramses, racing to catch up with him. Her long black hair was flowing in the wind and he thought that he had never seen anything…or anyone as beautiful.

Manal smiled broadly as she slowed her horse to a trot and then slowly rode up closer to Baako's side. She thought that she had never seen a man as handsome.

They heard the call to Morning Prayer coming from a distant minaret. The mists quickly dissipated as the sun rose higher.

Turning his head around, Baako kicked his heels against the horse's sides, let out a loud whoop, swiftly urging his horse into a gallop once again. Manal did the same and soon they were racing their shadows across the golden desert sands.

Their life together was just beginning. Within the past two weeks their lives, as well as those of Marcus, Valencia and Sebastian, had been changed forever in the most unexpected ways.

EPILOGUE

Inspector Ahmad Mohammadi, following up on merely a hunch and instinct, was able to get a confession from Sobek Salim for the murder of Manal's brother. There had been countless cigarette butts found at the murder site. Obviously the cigarettes used to torture the man. The same brand that Sobek had been smoking when the Inspector broke the news to the widow. An unusual brand imported into Egypt from Kuwait. The Inspector had also noticed the bruised knuckles on Sobek's hand. When confronted, the unapologetic perpetrator confessed, shrugging his shoulders, but claimed it as an "honor killing", common in Middle-Eastern countries.

The man was found guilty in a court of law and sentenced to hard labor and life in prison. However, an appeals court two months later reduced the sentence to fifteen years.

The case was not an exception. Reducing sentences in family violence cases isn't uncommon in Egypt.

Two months later, Baako Mustafa got the news he had been awaiting. He was offered the much-desired position of an Egyptologist at the prestigious Cairo Museum and granted the rights to the fieldwork of his choosing. Elated, he selected to pursue excavations in Memphis, at the site of the Step Pyramid of Djoser, in the Saqqara necropolis. He was certain there were more secrets to be unlocked there. And he was correct.

He and Manal Khalifa celebrated by getting married.

Manal soon became a popular, sought-after tour guide and was booked solid by tour operators for months.

In the years ahead, his and Manal's three inquisitive sons, Horus, Seth, and Ammon would follow them into the world of Egyptian archeology.

Six months after arriving back in the States from Egypt, Sebastian Reckling and a stewardess on Pam Am Airlines enjoyed their honeymoon in Europe after a whirlwind romance. He was never able to detect a falsehood in anything she had said about loving him forever. *This* marriage lasted. He was loyal to a fault. They never divorced. His heart would be lighter than a feather. Just barely…but lighter, nonetheless.

Nine months and three weeks after arriving back home from Egypt, Marcus and Valencia Darke became parents for the first time. Valencia thought she knew exactly when she became pregnant. Well, perhaps.

Perhaps was it on that loud, bumpy overnight train ride to Luxor that had them laughing hysterically as they made love?

Perhaps it was that night of the romantic full moon as they cruised down the river on the S.S. Sudan?

Or perhaps it was the champagne.

In any event, they named their handsome little son Niles.

A year and a half after returning from Egypt Marcus Darke had his latest bestseller. ANOTHER DARKE MYSTERY. His best written and most detail-oriented book yet according to all the literary critics… and to the delight of his publisher as well as his readers. Surrounded by stacks of his and Valencia's notes, dozens of photographs, and with the young Egyptologist's voice in his head, he had squirreled himself away and written a thrilling murder mystery that spanned millennia. A strange, tangled, unsolvable murder mystery unfolds in ancient Egypt as the Great Pyramid of Khufu was being built and, as totally improbable as it sounds, 5,000 years later a handsome young Egyptologist in modern day Cairo uncovers heretofore hidden scrolls of papyri with irrefutable clues and thus solves the crime.

The book was *Dedicated to Baako Mustafa…A Man Who Changed My Life Forever.*

Soon to be a major motion picture, with a cast of thousands, starring Yul Brynner, Jean Simmons, Richard Burton, and Joan Collins. In CinemaScope…and stereophonic sound!

Oh, yes…and the title? *A Perfect Murder Takes Time.*

Author's Notes

Facts & Fiction - Myths & Metaphors

I have been fascinated by Egypt and its mythology for decades. The research that I did for this book, therefore, was extensive. Some of what I've written here may be controversial to some. Please don't take offense in any way.

My fictional character, Baako Mustafa, was accurate with what he told Marcus and Valencia Darke, along with Sebastian Reckling. The *Ancient Egyptian Book of the Dead* can be considered the forefather of the Bible and Quran. And the 42 Negative Confessions in the Book of the Dead can be considered the forefather of the Law of Moses, more specifically, The Ten Commandments, predating them by centuries. These "confessions" were uttered by the recently deceased on their way to be judged either worthy or unworthy to proceed to a rewarding afterlife with Osiris.

Each confession was made to a different deity. I have omitted the particular deity after the first two in the listing here. I think you'll get the picture. I shall leave any opinions about them up to you, my readers, but I think you shall find the similarities to the Ten Commandments intriguing.

Hail, Usekh-nemmt, who comest forth from Anu, I have not committed sin.

Hail, Hept-Khet, who comest forth from Kher-aha, I have not committed robbery with violence.

...I have not stolen.

...I have not slain men and women.

...I have not stolen grain.

...*I have not purloined offerings.*
...*I have not stolen the property of God.*
...*I have not uttered lies.*
...*I have not carried away food.*
...*I have not uttered curses.*
...*I have not committed adultery.*
...*I have made none to weep.*
...*I have not eaten the heart.*
...*I have not attacked any man.*
...*I am not a man of deceit.*
...*I have not stolen cultivated land.*
...*I have not been an eavesdropper.*
...*I have not slandered any man.*
...*I have not been angry without just cause.*
...*I have not debauched the wife of any man.*
...*I have not polluted myself.*
...*I have terrorized none.*
...*I have not transgressed the law.*
...*I have not been wroth.*
...*I have not shut my ears to the words of truth.*
...*I have not blasphemed.*
...*I am not a man of violence.*
...*I have not been a stirrer up of strife.*
...*I have not acted with undue haste.*
...*I have not pried into matters.*
...*I have not multiplied my words in speaking.*
...*I have wronged no one.*
...*I have done no evil.*
...*I have not worked witchcraft against the king.*
...*I have never stopped the flow of water.*
...*I have never raised my voice.*
...*I have not cursed God.*
...*I have not acted with arrogance.*
...*I have not stolen the bread of the gods.*
...*I have not carried away the Khenfu cakes from the spirits of the dead.*
...*I have not snatched away the bread of the child, nor treated with contempt the god of my city.*
...*I have not slain the cattle belonging to the god.*

Baako Mustafa alluded to Marcus Darke and his friends about several other worldwide religions with death and resurrection scenarios. One in particular, of course, was Egyptian, relating the story of Isis and Osiris, which related back to the funerary texts and the *Book of the Dead*. Osiris played an extremely important role in ancient Egyptian religion and mythology. He was the god of fertility, agriculture, the afterlife, the dead, resurrection, life, and vegetation. As with the Wicked Witch of the West in modern times, on stage and screen, Osiris is depicted as a green-skinned deity. Green being the color of rebirth.

Murder, of course, then factored into his story. And it's a strange murder, to say the least. But was it a perfect murder? A bit over the top, to be sure, mythology notwithstanding.

Osiris was the first king of Egypt and he was much beloved. His brother, Seth, was jealous of him and plotted to kill him so that he could take the throne. Osiris, therefore, was murdered by his wicked brother. He was then cut up into several pieces and scattered about Egypt. Isis, the wife of Osiris, searched all over Egypt to find each part. She was able to find all but one of his parts...his genitalia, which had been eaten by fish. She then wrapped him up, partially mummy-wrapped at the legs. She turned herself into a large bird, flapping her wings to waft the breath of life back into his lungs, enabling him to return to life. He then became the judge and lord of the dead, and the underworld.

Mythology and religious doctrine can intertwine in wonderful and mysterious ways. I pass no judgment on neither mythology nor religion. What one person may believe in, another will scoff. Wars have been waged. Lives have been lost. Osiris and others will judge. Feathers are waiting to be weighed.

And then regarding the celebration of Christmas: December 25th is associated with the birth of many pagan gods, including Mithra, Horus, Hercules, Zeus, and Sol Invictus. The ancient Roman festival and holiday Saturnalia honoring the god Saturn, for example, once began on December 17th in the Julian calendar. It was later expanded with festivities until December 19th and, by the first century B.C., had been extended until December 23rd. It was a time of partying, banquets, and gift giving. The poet Catullus called it "the best of days".

Christianity imported many of these pagan myths and traditions into its own customs around 400 A.D.

And how about those magnificent Pyramids? Built by thousands of highly skilled laborers and farmers who could not work their fields during the annual flooding of the Nile. No, slaves did *not* build them, as Hollywood wants us to believe.

For centuries people have been baffled by their construction. How were the Egyptians, 4,000 + years ago, able to move those millions of limestone blocks, most weighing a ton or more, into position so precisely? They had no cranes, no power equipment. There were countless theories, but no verified conclusions. Until recently. Perhaps.

Rajan Hooda, an Indian-American with a PhD. from the University of Chicago, recently published a paper with what seems like a very plausible method that the Egyptians may have used. He is an archeology/history enthusiast who has spent a great part of his life trying to solve the Pyramid Puzzle. So, on October 11, 2024 (his 65th birthday), he willingly shared the results with the world.

If you are really interested (as I was), you are able to download a PDF of his multi-paged paper. Go to the website HTPWB.com. He explains, in great detail…even with diagrams…his theory. The name of this website is derived from the acronym for **H**ow **T**he **P**yramids **W**ere **B**uilt.

To be perfectly honest, I *still* do not understand it but it *is* fascinating nonetheless.

On a relatively minor note, but pivotal to all you nit-picking fact-checkers: The beginning of the Forensic Linguistics field didn't really kick into gear until 1963, leading to the creation of the Miranda Rights. Therefore, Sebastian Reckling was ahead of the times.

My wife, Gaylin, and I spent nearly three weeks in Egypt in October of 1990…two months after Saddam Hussein had attacked Kuwait. Could have been scary times. A few of our friends thought we should cancel our trip, but I said, "If TWA is still flying in, so are we!" We never encountered any danger but, that being said, two weeks after we got back home a busload of German tourists were gunned down by a small band of terrorists on the highway from Alexandria to Cairo. That was on the very same route on which we had traveled.

Although we didn't *actually* do it, it felt as though we must have visited every tomb and temple from Alexandria to Abu Simbel. The unforgettable trip was exhilarating, to say the least.

We had a marvelous and beautiful twenty-seven-year-old Egyptologist as our guide. Yes, her name was Manal although, for the life of me, I cannot remember her last name. She brought their ancient history alive for us and the memories are still as vivid today. She wore an intoxicating light perfume. I may have been smitten.

I took some liberties, however, with a few minor details. We, too, sailed down the Nile for a few days. Maybe not on such a luxurious vessel as the SS Sudan, but it was delightful nonetheless. I made it sound that one could simply disembark the boat and walk casually into the Valley of the Kings in just a few moments. Not so. Tourists need to be either taxied or bussed into that wondrous site, which was several miles from the river's edge.

Just like Baako and his American trio, we also took the overnight train from Cairo to Luxor. By that time, however, if memory serves me well, Egyptian laws had changed and alcoholic beverages were being served in the Club Car. But it *was* extremely smoky…seemed like everyone smoked in Egypt…and we didn't stay in the lounge area for very long. And, yes, the train was *exceedingly* noisy, bumpy and jerky. The two meals served, dinner and breakfast, would never win any culinary awards, that's for damn sure! But it was a fun experience nonetheless.

As much as we learned while were there, Egyptologists and archaeologists are *still* uncovering secrets of ancient Egypt and the life of the pharaohs to this day. The largest collection of nonfiction books in my personal library in our home deals with that fascinating country.

We stood on a balcony of the venerable old hotel, the Mena House Oberoi, overlooking the Great Pyramids. That's the Pyramid of Khufu on the left, the one from which Reckless nearly fell. It is the oldest and tallest of the Pyramids.

While one might expect that the Pyramids are *way* out there somewhere in the desert, actually the city of Giza is practically at their base. Traffic and camels abound together. It is, indeed, a surprising feeling to be at the base of the Great Pyramids and see a vast metropolis in sight and within hearing distance.

Gaylin, standing at the base of the Pyramid of Khufu. Those blocks of limestone are *huge*!

Although a dog has recently been spotted cavorting and barking at birds on top on the Pyramid of Khufu, climbing to the top (for humans) is now *strictly* forbidden. However, visitors *are* permitted to go into the Pyramid and climb up to one of the burial chambers. It was a very steep, dark, narrow climb. I went only partway up, I'm claustrophobic, but Gaylin went all the way up into the King's Chamber. A challenge I declined.

A silly little piece of Egyptian trivia: Cleopatra lived closer in time to the invention of the iPhone than to the construction of the Great Pyramids of Giza. The Pyramids were already over 2,500 years old by the time she was born in 69 B.C.

And just to set the record straight in case you might not know it already: Although Cleopatra was the last pharaoh of Egypt, she was not Egyptian. She was of Macedonian Greek descent and had little to no Egyptian blood. She was born in Egypt to Ptolemy XII, the ruling Ptolemaic pharaoh.

Of course, we did the touristy thing and rode camels around in the sand of the Western Desert for a while.

And, yes, we did give the camel's owner "Bakshish...Bakshish!"

Our guide, Manal, with a young falcon on her arm. Perhaps it might be a distant relative to the great falcon-headed god Horus.

There were many, many things we learned and saw on *our* journey that I simply could not include in Baako's itinerary for this book.

Walking through the massive colonnades at the Temple of Karnak. Perhaps this was where Valencia Darke encountered the cobra. Fortunately, we did not.

We took a stroll along the Avenue of the Sphinxes, which connects Luxor Temple, behind my wife, with Karnak Temple to *my* back. My wife is taking the pharaoh's pose so typical of much of the statuary. There once were two of those tall red granite obelisks flanking the entrance to the temple. In a diplomatic gift to France, the obelisk that would have stood on the right was sent to Paris in 1829.

Four years after the previous photo was taken, when we were in Paris celebrating our 30th wedding anniversary, we saw the gifted missing obelisk that now stands tall in the Place de la Concorde. Once again, my wife is striking the pharaonic pose.

While Marcus, Valencia and Sebastian were unable to get to see it during their interrupted journey, here I stand at Abu Simbel.

There are two temples at this site. The large one, behind where I'm standing, is the Temple of Ramesses II, with four colossal statues of the Pharaoh guarding the entrance. There is a smaller temple off to the right, the Temple of the goddess Hathor and Queen Nefertari, the Pharaoh's favorite wife. Hathor is the ancient Egyptian goddess of love, joy, beauty, and fertility. Appropriate, because Nefertari translates to "the most beautiful one".

Fact: In one of the greatest challenges of archaeological engineering history, between 1964 and 1968 the entire site was carefully cut into large chunks, dismantled, lifted and precisely reassembled higher and further back from the Nile River. This was done to save the temples from the rising water of Lake Nasser as a result of the construction of the Aswan High Dam.

A multinational team of archeologists and engineers, under the banner of UNESCO, worked together to accomplish this truly awe-inspiring feat.

The cost, then, was a staggering $40 million, equivalent in today's money to approximately $400 million. Well worth the money spent.

My wife is standing in front of the Step Pyramid of Djoser, in Memphis. This was the very first pyramid built in Egypt, constructed between 2670 – 2650 B.C.

We brought home from Egypt an excellent papyrus reproduction depicting a *very* small portion of the Book of the Dead, my personal favorite part. This is the judgment scene. The deceased is being led to the scale by the jackal-headed god, Anubis. The seated judges above in the scene have listened to his Forty-two Negative Confessions, and the ibis-headed god Thoth, is waiting to see if the deceased's heart is lighter than the feather. The goddess/beast, Ammit, Devourer of the Dead, looks to the scribe, Thoth, and awaits the judgment to see if she gets to eat the heart which will send the deceased to an extremely unpleasant afterlife. The judged virtuous deceased is then ushered by the falcon-headed god Horus to join the resurrected powerful Osiris in a glorious afterlife.

Our first names, in Egyptian hieroglyphics, were hand-painted in the cartouches on either end of the papyrus.

When the time comes for *us* to be judged, I have no doubt that my wife's heart will be lighter than the feather. Mine? I'm not so sure.

ACKNOWLEDGMENTS

When I self-published my very first book, *Horse Scents*, at the age of 78, I honestly thought "One and done". It was a fun process and a real ego trip. No great expectations were there. I didn't anticipate that it would sell in the millions (it didn't, of course...nowhere near). With no marketing done whatsoever aside from me blasting its publication to my Facebook Friends and family, and announcing its publication to our Zumba class at our gym, I got some modest sales and a readership. That first book cried out for a sequel and it got one the following year, *Stable Affairs*.

Well...the writing bug had bitten at that point, and here I am, nearing the age of 83 and this is Book #8.

I sincerely...truly...honestly...gratefully thank all my faithful readers, few though they may be, for the encouragement. The invitations to speak at various Book Clubs have been additional ego boosters and loads of fun.

Hopefully my readers have learned some things along the way. I do a *lot* of research when I write these things, and try to include some actual pieces of history. Some of which has been surprising to many. I have yet to hear from any fact-checkers that my facts are incorrect or erroneous. Maybe they're just being polite.

My boldest, toughest critic, best editor and proofreader throughout this entire process has been my beautiful, faithful, loving wife of 60 years (yes, 60!!), Gaylin. I've given her fits with my promises of "No more writing. No more books." Promises broken. But she remains the best friend I have ever had. She has been the absolute best travel companion and navigator anyone could hope for as we journeyed all around the globe.

She has, indeed, changed *my* life forever.

Printed in the United States
by Baker & Taylor Publisher Services